UNLOCKING LIES

Keys to Love, Book Three

Kennedy Layne

Dedication

Jeffrey—Simply put…I love you.

Cole—It's so hard to believe this is your senior year of high school. We are so proud of all you've accomplished, and we will be there cheering you on as you enter college to pursue your dreams. We love you!

Secrets and lies have a way of weaving a deadly web.

Returning home from his last deployment shouldn't have been complicated, but Jace Kendall was immediately drawn into a murder investigation that hits a little too close to home. The last thing he should be doing was reigniting old passions that should have been kept buried, but he's never been a guy who plays by the rules.

Shae has suffered for twelve years without knowing why her sister disappeared. The long-awaited answers are now within reach, and she'll have no choice but to trust the one man who knows more than he's telling.

It isn't long before Jace and Shae are lost in the mystery of solving a case that's long gone cold. When they find the answers they've been looking for, a darkness is unveiled that will leave one of them in the crosshairs of a psychopath.

CHAPTER ONE

Twelve years ago…

LIGHTNING STREAKED ACROSS the sky in multiple jagged forks overhead.

The waning flash eventually morphed into an ominous rumble of thunder, creating a malevolent omen as it continued to sing its song throughout the collapsing resonance.

Emma Irwin bit back the sob that threatened to escape her throat, causing her breath to hitch.

She didn't want to die today.

The hulking man standing in front of her abruptly lunged forward, causing her to cry out in alarm. She instinctively stumbled backwards and somehow managed to twist around without falling.

Emma ran for her life, and she didn't look back.

There was only one path she could take that would lead her to safety. Under normal circumstances, she would have been able to navigate these woods like the back of her hand. Now? Terror flooded her bloodstream, making it nearly impossible for her to formulate a plan.

The thunderstorm above all but descended the forest into darkness after each flash. Without night vision, the footing amongst the roots crisscrossing the forest floor became treacherous. She had to keep an arm raised as she ran through the trees to prevent the low hanging branches from slamming into her face. Her hands were already bleeding from her previous fall, but fortunately, there was no pain as a result of the endorphins.

She couldn't afford the distraction her pain would cause.

How could this be happening?

Emma wanted to stop and scream at him at the top of her lungs. She'd known him her whole life. She had trusted him, and yet she didn't doubt that he would kill her with no more remorse than he would experience by putting down a game animal.

All she needed to do was make it to Seventh Street. If she could reach the edge of town, someone would help her.

Would anyone believe her? Was any of this even remotely plausible?

She was a teenager. It was her word against…

Light!

The streetlamp was barely visible, but it was there ahead of her just up the gradual slope. The blazing beacon provided her hope.

The drizzling rain became more of a steadier stream the closer she got to the edge of the woods. Unadulterated fear kept up her forward momentum until her ankle boot slipped on a small pile of loose leaves.

Emma hit the ground so hard that her lungs emptied of any air that may have been left in her body after running so far at such a fast pace. She opened her mouth to drag in what oxygen she could, but her lungs seemed incapable of working. Her brain was screaming at her to get up and move or else she would die.

This was it.

She was going to die here, because she couldn't overcome the fear.

Little by little, her straining muscles relaxed to the point where she was able to suck in a small measure of oxygen. It was enough to stop the flashing lights that had started to circulate in her line of vision. In their place, images of her sister began to materialize.

Would Shae miss her?

Emma didn't want their last words to be those of hate. She'd said some awful things to her sister this afternoon all because Shae had gotten the car tonight.

"It's not fair!" Emma screamed at her mom, stomping out of the kitchen and wishing there was a door to slam. All she wanted to do was hit something or someone. It didn't help that Shae was coming down the staircase with an amused smirk on her face. "Why did you have to be the older one? How come you always get to be first?"

"I don't know why you're so upset." Shae shrugged as if this night was no big deal. Emma bit her tongue as she passed her sister on the steps. Their mother was most likely listening to them in the kitchen, and the last thing Emma needed was to get grounded before the biggest bonfire of the year. "You get the car all week long while I'm at college. Besides, you got to use it last weekend."

"No," Emma argued, unable to stop herself. She spun around on the second step to face Shae, who had already reached the landing. "I only got to use the car on Friday night. Remember? You went into the city all day on Saturday."

"I'm in college, Emma. I'm not allowed a vehicle on campus, so I should get the car two nights out of the week. Those days just happen to fall on the weekends." Shae crossed her arms like she did when she was trying to make a point and look all mature. Just because she was in college didn't mean that she was an adult. "What's the big deal, anyway? You can have one of your friends pick you up. It's safe that way."

"Brynn's car is in the shop, and you know that Julie doesn't have access to one." Why should Emma have to explain why she wanted the car? "You know what? Take the car. I don't care anymore."

"Good, because I am taking it. It's my turn."

"I hate you!"

A tear ran down Emma's right cheek, though the rain washed it away. She didn't hate her sister. Shae was everything Emma wanted to be.

Lightning lit up the sky overhead, illuminating her surroundings.

He was gone.

He was nowhere to be seen.

Emma was finally breathing again, though her heart was beating hard against her chest. She scrambled to her feet and did a full turn to scan her immediate surroundings. She was alone in the dark, but something told her he would appear out of nowhere her if she didn't keep moving.

She took off once again for Seventh Street, relief washing over her as she finally reached the paved road. Not once did she think of slowing down her pace, though she did veer to the right so that she could follow the road that would lead her past the cemetery and toward the back end of town. She'd take the shortcut to her house from there.

It was then she saw the silhouette standing on the other side of the road blocking her path.

It was him.

That's why he hadn't come upon her when she'd fallen on the leaves. He'd somehow run ahead to cut her off before she could get home.

Emma had no choice but to run back toward the woods. There was no holding back the sobs that had been trying to escape. Why was he doing this to her? What had she done to him?

It was hard to see through her tears, but she ran blindly through the trees nonetheless. She didn't follow any path, and she certainly never expected two arms to reach out of the darkness to save her. They embraced her warmly, and she even heard the soothing words that everything would be alright.

She was safe.

Emma broke down, holding onto the strong arms so that she wouldn't sink to the ground.

"H-he's coming," Emma managed to say, trying to warn whoever had saved her. Was it Billy? Lance Kendall? Chad Schaeffer? It didn't matter. "He's right behind me and—"

Something was wrong.

Emma furiously blinked her tears away and looked up at her savior.

Only she was mistaken.

No one was here to save her.

All hope vanished. She didn't understand how it happened, but the man she was running from hadn't been the one standing in the middle of Seventh Street.

He'd been waiting for her in the shadows all along.

CHAPTER TWO

Present day…

"I SEE DAD'S been by to visit."

Jace Kendall couldn't help but smile in sadness at the lone tea rose laying on his mother's tombstone. Lilacs had been Mary Kendall's favorite, but they were out of season this late in August. This particular tea rose, called Darlow's Enigma, no doubt came from one of the bushes she'd planted years ago in the front of their family home. The fragrant blooms lasted all summer long and gave the whole front yard a wonderful aroma with each successive breeze. One of the best climbing roses on the market, his mother's trellis had long since been overrun.

"It looks as if he's been taking care of your gardening. Noah said Dad's thumb is finally showing a bit of green."

Jace's own thumb was pricked when he examined the small sprig, only then remembering Darlow's Enigma had one major bad attribute. Their many thousands of thorns were razor sharp. Their beauty could cut a person to the bone.

He wanted to say more to his mom, but the words wouldn't come. Instead, he looked up from his mother's engraved name and took in his immediate surroundings.

Blyth Lake.

His childhood hometown.

In the twelve years he'd been gone, there hadn't been one occasion when he returned on leave where he hadn't driven straight to his parents' house…until now.

"You have an amazing view." Jace was glad his father had purchased this particular plot, seeing as it was on the back edge of the graveyard and overlooking a rolling field of wildflowers. There was even a large white oak that provided shade from the hot sun. He pictured himself and his brothers chasing each other through the field as their mother and father walked hand in hand. Their sister had always remained within a few yards of their dad and never ventured too far. "Dad's in the process of making a wooden bench that will go perfect underneath that tree."

Jace took a deep breath, closed his eyes, and then exhaled slowly. He tried to compose his emotions. He honestly hadn't thought returning home without his mom to greet him on the front porch would be quite this hard. He'd stopped at the entrance in town, wanting so bad to make that left turn…but he couldn't bring himself to do it. He'd known he would be coming here to see her grave for the first time since the funeral.

He'd driven straight down Main Street until he'd hit Seventh. The entrance to the cemetery didn't feel like much of a warm welcome, but he took solace in the fact that his mother was at peace. She'd wanted that for her children, as well.

Jace suffered quite a bit through his time in the service. The Corps didn't find itself in the vacation spots around the world too often. He had served his country, and now he believed he was entitled to pursue the happiness that had eluded him thus far.

"I'm sure you heard about the crazy events that have been happening this past summer." Jace cleared his throat before kneeling, not wanting his voice to carry over the slight breeze. He didn't see anyone in close proximity, but this was still a private conversation. "I can't believe that Noah found a body inside the wall of his new house. I mean, what are the odds of that kind of insanity happening here in Blyth Lake? He always did have to be the one to stir up trouble in the neighborhood."

He pictured Mary Kendall wagging her finger his way, letting him know that he ought to be nicer to his younger brother. Now, he had to chide himself. It hadn't always been easy being the middle child of five, but he wouldn't change a second of his childhood in this rural paradise they called home. Life here was so much simpler than the breakneck pace at which the rest of the world ran. Time stood still here amongst the live oaks.

Mitch and Gwen were the oldest of the Kendall siblings, whereas Noah and Lance were the younger. Jace had been the pivot point, smackdab in the middle. The experts always said that the middle child was the peacemaker. That wasn't the case in the Kendall clan. Their sister, Gwen, had taken that particular role. He imagined that she took on the responsibility just because she couldn't stand having her brothers fight over stupid shit repeatedly.

Had it not been for his mom, Jace most likely would have been an oddball loner who eventually turned into an uptight asshole. Mary Kendall had made sure he was the youngest of the first three and the oldest of the last three. There wasn't a moment in time where he'd ever felt out of place.

"I do miss you, Mama." Jace was out of one-on-one time. He'd learned early on that privacy was the first casualty of having a large family, and seeing Lance's old F150 through the wrought iron fence was just another reminder. His baby brother pulled into the cemetery parking lot, leaving Jace to wonder how that old truck was still even running. "Lance couldn't have given me two more minutes alone with you, could he? I know, I know. Be nice."

Jace leaned his palm against the cool grass, lowering himself to the ground. He might as well make himself comfortable. Lance would have to walk halfway through the graveyard to reach him. He wasn't about to make it easy for his baby brother to horn in on this moment.

His mother's wagging finger once again materialized in his mind.

"Oh, Mom. Trust me, he could use the exercise."

Lance slammed the driver's side door shut before shading his eyes to determine if Jace would decide to head his way.

Not a chance, buddy.

Jace rested a forearm over his knee, enjoying the fact that Lance was muttering curses under his breath as he started hiking up the small rise. He didn't realize his mini rant carried across the cemetery as well as it did. It wasn't long until he was standing in front of their mother's tombstone.

There were times in life that Jace's siblings surprised him…this moment included. Lance lowered himself next to Jace, and they sat in silence for a good five minutes. Oddly so, it was actually nice to have the company of a family member here on this midsummer's day.

"Welcome home," Lance finally said, not even bothering to glance Jace's way.

"It's good to be back," Jace replied, picking at the grass by his side. He might as well fess up. "I wasn't quite ready to pull up the drive, you know what I mean?"

"You don't have to explain yourself to me. Been there myself." Lance lifted his shades until they were resting on top of his head. "The day I drove into town, Dad came strolling out onto the front porch wearing his barbeque apron and carrying a spatula in his hand. Let's just say there was an adjustment process."

"Everyone already at the house waiting on me?" Jace wasn't

about to get emotional. He'd been there and done that on the day of Mary Kendall's funeral. He sighed in resignation as he tossed the blades of grass back down onto the ground. "I was hoping to come home quietly, without any kind of fanfare and such."

"Yeah, that's not gonna happen. Noah and Reese were in the kitchen mixing a massive tossed garden salad when I left, and Brynn was leaving the Cavern when you drove past."

"Brynn threw me under the bus, didn't she?" Jace should have known that someone would spot him, but it wasn't like everyone in town knew he owned a Range Rover. He could all but guarantee that was rectified by the time he'd reached Seventh Street. The word was out. "Dad said the two of you reconnected in the month that you've been home. You don't waste time, do you, brother?"

"She's the one for me, Jace." Lance didn't even bother to hide his goofy grin. He and Brynn had been involved back in high school. Apparently, those old embers had been rekindled with a bit of effort. "She moved in with me last week, as a matter of fact."

"What is it with you and Noah buying houses without taking your time to look around town? I'm absolutely certain you could have chosen better." Jace could understand Lance doing something so impulsive, but Noah? That didn't make any sense. "Let's face it, the choices the two of you made wasn't the brightest, now were they?"

"Noah found the body in his wall," Lance pointed out, sitting up a bit straighter. "I only found pictures of teenage girls who were either abducted or murdered. We must have hit the supernatural lottery with those odds."

"Get up, you idiot," Jace directed, pushing himself off the ground and dusting himself off. He had on a pair of his favorite jeans and one of his button-down shirts with the sleeves rolled up to his forearms. He always did have better taste in clothes than Lance. "I'm not talking about a serial killer roaming around Blyth Lake while we sit next to Mom's grave."

"It's not like she doesn't already know what's been going on," Lance muttered, catching up with Jace after a few steps. "Maybe she'll give us a sign. She never did like people thinking bad of us Kendalls or screwing with our hometown's image."

"I lay sole blame on Noah. Can you imagine finding a body in the drywall of your house? He has the reverse *Midas Touch*. Everything he touches turns to shit."

"Don't tell Noah, but I already thanked Mom for not letting it be me." Lance put his sunglasses back onto the bridge of his nose. "Imagine Noah's surprise when the body turned out to be Sophia Morton, and not Emma."

Jace figured everyone in Blyth Lake was surprised the body belonged to someone else besides Emma Irwin. The seventeen-year-old girl went missing close to twelve years ago. Her abduction was the biggest mystery this town had ever heard of or seen since. No one knew if she was alive, dead, or abducted by those famous probing aliens.

In all seriousness, that theory had been proposed by Wylie Tilmadge. Good old Wylie used to live on the outskirts of town and had been a favorite with the media back in the day. He had really been out there on the edge.

As for Sophia Morton, it was Jace's understanding that she had been a young girl who lived in the nearby town of Heartland, Ohio. The small town was located around thirty miles to the east of Blyth Lake. The only connection between Emma and Sophia had been the fact that they'd both attended summer camp together…the same camp Lance had attended the summer before he shipped off to boot camp.

"So, let me get this straight," Jace said, figuring he might as well be up to speed on current events before driving home and being thrust into the middle of the latest edition of an old story. "The police believe that Sophia Morton was murdered by the same person who kidnapped Emma? Weren't those cases a year apart? I would think that the two events would be considered unrelated until proven otherwise. I mean, it's a stretch, isn't it?"

"You would think, but then how did Sophia's body end up here in Blyth Lake? Not to mention I found pictures in the basement of my house that do, in fact, prove otherwise." Lance and Jace finally reached their vehicles, but neither of them made an attempt to get behind the wheels. "Emma and Sophia's photographs were both in that pile of victims, Jace. It wasn't a coincidence. Someone targeted those girls."

"And what about all the other teenagers who were photographed?" Jace wasn't sure he wanted to know, but somehow his two younger brothers had managed to get involved in an active, honest to God homicide investigation. Now that couldn't be a coincidence. "Have the police located any of them or their relatives?"

Lance leaned against the side of his truck before rubbing a hand over his face in an attempt to delay his answer. This couldn't be good.

"Dad figured he'd told you enough bad news in one phone call, so he might have left off a few details."

"Like what?" Jace didn't like returning to town blind in one eye. He liked being prepared, and not being handled. Leaving the service hadn't changed that part of his personality. "Spit it out, for Christ's sake. I'm already coming home to find my younger brothers living on their own broken-down farms and playing house with their dream girls. Is anyone pregnant yet?"

Jace didn't have to explain that he was talking about Brynn

Mercer and Reese Woodward. Granted, he could understand Lance and Brynn getting back together. They'd been an item for most of their high school tenure. That wasn't much of a stretch, but the fact that Noah was involved with Reese Woodward was blowing Jace's mind. What the hell had they put in the water since he was last here? It had to be poisoned.

Reese had come to town seeking answers about Sophia's disappearance, somehow connecting Sophia to Emma before anyone else did. It came to light that Reese and Sophia were cousins. Honestly, Jace wasn't sure he wanted to know all the particulars now that he was home. At this point, he was thinking it might have been smarter for him to have delayed his homecoming and let all this crazy just blow over. Lance's next statement confirmed it.

"Whitney Bell was abducted from her dad's house just a couple of weeks ago." Lance shook his head in regret. "The police have fairly convincing evidence that she's dead."

Jace let that bit of news sink in as he reconciled past events with current.

He definitely should have delayed his homecoming. Hell, maybe he could sneak out of town before anyone else noticed he was here. *Oh, that's right.* It was a little too late for that.

"You're telling me that the person who abducted Emma twelve years ago and murdered Sophia Morton eleven years ago is the same individual who killed Whitney Bell a couple of weeks ago?" Jace briefly thought about getting in his truck and driving out of town anyway. The only thing that stopped him was the vision of his dad standing on the front porch in his barbeque apron. "That is some crazy shit, brother."

"You want to know what's even crazier yet?"

Not really, but Jace had never been able to put a muzzle on Lance in the past. He doubted he could do so now.

"We have an active serial killer in Blyth Lake, and he's drag-ging—either by happenstance or with intent—all of us Kendalls into the middle of this investigation." Lance shot Jace a look of warning. "Watch your back, brother. We got a homicidal maniac itching to do some kind of harm to those we love."

CHAPTER THREE

SHAE IRWIN GRIPPED the steering wheel of her Jeep Grand Cherokee for the umpteenth time. Maybe she should start the engine, turn her SUV around, and head back the way she'd come. It wasn't like her presence here in Blyth Lake would change anything for anyone.

"Stop being a coward," Shae muttered to herself, glancing in the rearview mirror. Instantly, she wished she hadn't done that. Her bloodshot eyes only reminded her that she hadn't been sleeping too well lately. "Get a grip, Shae."

Without giving herself time to second guess her decision, she took the keys from the ignition and grabbed her purse from the passenger side seat. It was time she faced her demons instead of remaining on the same old road that led anywhere but home.

Yes, Blyth Lake *was* her hometown. It didn't matter that she and her parents had turned tail and run away after Emma's disappearance. They'd even lost touch with neighbors and old friends that the family had for years…quite on purpose. Anything to wipe out the painful memories of their loss.

Shae stared at the front entrance of Tiny's Cavern before glancing down Main Street. Nothing here had changed in the twelve years she'd been gone. Most of the old businesses that lined both sides of the street were still here, unlike most of the rest of middle America. The town council controlled what business came to town and who received a license to operate in most of the county. They'd even tied up the water rights and kept the big chain stores out of town. But a few of the established storefronts had been swapped out for newer ones. No longer was renting videos a thing, nor was having a small credit union in demand when one could do everything at the main bank.

The past was vanishing little by little, and they'd all allowed it to slip away one piece at a time. Hell, they even had a local High-Speed Internet Service Provider here in town, right across from the same old Ben Franklin Pharmacy.

"Shae Irwin?"

She'd all but been standing in the middle of the street. A quick look over her shoulder revealed Calvin Arlos—a man who the police had suspected might be involved in her sister's disappearance.

Then again, so was everyone else in this accursed town.

"Hi, Mr. Arlos," Shae greeted softly, dropping her keys in her purse as she rounded the back end of her vehicle. He ran the hardware store a few blocks over and used to give her a lollipop every time she accompanied her dad into the shop. She didn't believe for a second this man was involved with what happened to Emma, but the Smith & Wesson model 360 loaded with 158 grain .357 magnum Federal Hydra-Shok rounds sitting in her purse assured her personal security all the same. It was amazing how a person changed after a tragedy. "How are you feeling? I heard you were in the hospital recently."

Shae might have purposefully maintained her distance from the residents of Blyth Lake, but that didn't mean she didn't check in from time to time. Mr. Arlos had been taken in for questioning by a detective by the name of Kendrick all because Calvin had taken a few pictures at a summer camp her sister had attended a few months before her abduction. The pictures weren't even his idea. He'd taken them for inclusion in the local community business association's brochure. Back then, the camp had been a part of the town's business collective.

The stress of the whole investigation had been too much for Calvin. He'd suffered a heart attack. Honestly, Shae was surprised to see him out and about so soon.

"Oh, you know how it is. These people around here make a big deal out of the inanest thing possible." Calvin gingerly stepped off the curb, seemingly surprised when Shae lifted up on her tiptoes to kiss his cheek. "My ticker just needed a little fine tuning, if you know what I mean."

"I'm glad to hear that it was nothing," Shae replied with an understanding smile, figuring it was best to go along with him. "Are you still fishing up at the lake? Anything biting?"

"I was, though I've been under house arrest for the last few weeks. I've still got the trolling motor battery on the trickle charger."

For a brief moment, Shae believed Calvin meant he was literally under house arrest. His throaty laugh and how he held his chest to ease the ache from his recent surgery proved otherwise. He was referring to his doctor's orders.

"I thought I'd hit up the Cavern this evening and show everyone that I'm not some weak-kneed old man who's about to kick the bucket." Calvin adjusted his John Deere baseball cap, still seemingly a bit unnerved to be around her. "I'm sorry that your family has to relive the pain from losing Emma. I hope they catch that stupid son of a bitch who's been terrorizing all those young girls. Would you be interested in an escort, if you're heading inside?"

Terrorizing was nothing compared to murder, but Shae understood what Calvin meant in his expression of remorse. She'd come to town for that very reason.

She wanted justice.

"I appreciate that, Mr. Arlos."

Shae couldn't bring herself to go into Tiny's Cavern quite yet. It was still relatively early—maybe around seven o'clock in the evening—but it was a Friday night, after all. The whole town would be here within the next couple of hours. Everyone and their father would be hitting this bar.

Unfortunately, her temporary sleeping arrangements for her stay was the apartment above the Cavern. She'd have to go inside and see Brynn Mercer for the key eventually, but not right this second.

"I've been driving most of the day, so I'm going to walk to the diner for a bite to eat."

"You be careful," Calvin warned, his gaze leaving her and scanning Main Street. "Keep your head on a swivel. After what happened to Whitney, you'd think the town board would add more deputies to the department. People need to feel safe in their own neighborhood."

Shae nodded her agreement, but she wisely remained silent. She wasn't ready to talk about Whitney Bell or the fact that another murder had taken place.

Honestly, she wasn't so sure she was ready to be back here in Blyth Lake.

Shae looked both ways before crossing Main Street, stepping up onto the sidewalk away from the few oncoming vehicles looking for a parking spot. The bar's small lot was full, though that wasn't unusual for a Friday night. Main Street would have cars lined up by the night's end. Some from the bar, and others from the two-screen movie theater down the street.

Neon lights denoted both of the nighttime attractions here in Blyth Lake, more so for the theater. The owner had just finished a renovation, and the place was lit up like a mini-city.

There wasn't one car, truck, or SUV parked along Main Street that she recognized right off, but then again, she'd been gone for a very long time.

Or not long enough.

"Jack." Shae would have run into the man had she not been trying to see who was inside the diner by craning her neck. He'd come barreling out the glass door as if the building were on fire, not caring who was in his way. He always was a little self-centered, even when he was younger. "It's been a long while."

It was really wrong of her to experience a streak of pleasure as Jack Stuart seemed a bit speechless at her presence. Bygones should be bygones, but the memory of him making fun of Emma when she got her braces was hard to forget. His stymie now provided a little satisfaction.

"Shae, I didn't know you were back in town." Jack awkwardly leaned in for a hug, as if he wasn't sure how to greet her. A handshake would have been fine, but she followed suit. They were in a small town, after all. "It's good to see you."

They were still standing on the sidewalk, but Shae could sense each heavy stare from those who were left inside the diner. She never thought returning to her hometown would be easy, but this was downright awkward. Were they all staring at her because they expected her to start screaming and losing her shit?

"Please tell me that there's still a slice of Annie's apple pie left in the bakery case." Shae was going to make this exchange as normal as she could muster, given the circumstances. "I've been driving all day thinking of her homemade apple pies."

"I don't know," Jack admitted reluctantly with a crooked smile. "I was just saying hi to my mom before meeting up with Beth Ann over at the Cavern."

That's right. Brynn had mentioned in their last phone call that Jack was dating Beth Ann.

"Well, I won't keep you then," Shae said, meaning every word. "I'm starving, but give Beth Ann my best. I'm sure I'll see the two of you shortly, seeing as I'm staying in Brynn's old studio apartment above the bar."

Calvin Arlos being somewhat shocked at stumbling into her in town was one thing. After all, he'd been holed up at home and recovering from open heart surgery. Jack, on the other hand, was something entirely different. He seemed thrown for a complete loop at the sight of her knowing smile.

Brynn hadn't told a soul that Shae was returning home.

Oh, this should be illuminating.

She was grateful for the small favor. The Irwin family had been the talk of the town for far too long, and she certainly didn't want to add to the local gossip mill. The opportunity to catch everyone unprepared for her appearance had its own benefits. Unfortunately, keeping the residents in the dark about her return also meant uncomfortable meetings such as this one. She might as well have spilt the beans regardless, especially considering that Calvin was currently announcing her arrival to the entire bar.

"Yeah, I heard Brynn had moved in with Lance," Jack replied, most likely because he wasn't sure what else to say. "I'm sure I'll see you around then. Are you visiting or are you staying for a while?"

"Just visiting," Shae replied honestly, not sure she'd ever come back to Blyth Lake once Emma's case was solved. "Have a good night, Jack."

Shae didn't give him time to ask her any other questions. She shouldered past him and opened the door, covering her wince as the bell above her began to ring.

"Shae Irwin, I don't believe my eyes!" Molly Stuart came around the counter wiping her hands on the white apron tied around her waist. Shae didn't believe for a second that the woman's hands had anything on them. Everyone had been waiting eagerly for Shae to walk inside. "Aren't you absolutely beautiful. Cassie, come here! Shae's come home!"

Shae managed a smile as she was engulfed in Molly's embrace. It wasn't long before the other patrons began standing from their tables and coming over to greet her. It was as if the town's welcome wagon had been rolled out.

Harlan Whitmore and his wife had been very good friends with her parents, as were Chester and Stella Mayer. The couples used to have a weekly game of Euchre, and probably still did. Shae hadn't meant to make anyone uncomfortable, least of all these few couples who had always been friends to the family.

Yes, she was well aware that Harlan had been called in for questioning due to his connection to the properties linked to the so-called serial killer. Not even Detective Kendrick had proven to her that scenario existed one hundred percent. As for Harlan, he'd sold both properties to the Kendalls. She chalked everyone's involvement up to this point as a coincidence. Every loose connection to this case was circumstantial.

"How are your parents holding up under all this scrutiny?" Harlan asked after everyone had settled down some. Molly had gone back around the counter to fetch a fresh pot of coffee, while some of the others returned to their food before it got cold. "I, um, I hope you know that I had nothing to do with your sister's disappearance. You and your family mean the—"

"Harlan, it never occurred to me that you were." Shae stressed her reassurance by resting a hand on his arm. "I didn't come to town to accuse anyone of harming Emma or anyone else."

It was rare that Shae ever spoke her sister's name aloud. She gave Harlan a small smile to cover up her misstep.

"It's been so long since then. We've gone without answers for so long that I thought maybe being here might jog my memory of what happened back during that time. I'm sure everyone knows I've been in contact with Detective Kendrick, but those long-distance calls just weren't enough for me anymore." Shae shrugged in the futility of her objective. She was technically here for selfish reasons, because no answer would bring back her sister. "Go on and enjoy your dinner. I'm sure we'll have time to catch up once I've established a foothold."

It was apparent Harlan wanted to ask her more questions, but he thought better of it as he joined his wife and the other couple. She hoped her words reassured him that she had no hard feelings that he had been dragged into this investigation just like so many others. Technically, it wasn't even Emma's case.

Detective Kendrick was investigating Sophia Morton's death. Emma was still listed as a cold case.

Shae was tired. She should have gathered enough courage and gone into the Cavern the minute she'd arrived in town. She could have simply asked Brynn for the key while avoiding eye contact with the other patrons and then slept until tomorrow morning. That would have been the smart thing to do. Now, she had no choice but to take a back booth and eat a piece of pie and wash it down with a hot cup of tea.

It was hard not to look around for Cassie Osburn. The daughter of the infamous Annie's Diner owner had been sentenced to community service for her role in trying to drive Reese Woodward out of town. That just went to show that making assumptions could get anyone into trouble fairly easily. Shae wanted to be sure before she acted.

Cassie's criminal woes didn't seem to be hurting business, though. A third of the tables still had diners, and Shae could safely bet a hundred dollars that every seat had been occupied an hour ago. Nightlife in Blyth Lake was almost nonexistent, so the fact that Brynn started to host live bands at Tiny's Cavern had everyone going early to vie for a decent table.

Shae set her purse with its deadly contents on the far seat and slid it across the faux red leather. Her back protested the position, though her taut muscles from the long drive most definitely appreciated the small walk from her car to the diner. She was really glad the meeting she scheduled with Detective Kendrick wasn't until tomorrow afternoon. She would need to catch up on her sleep, if possible.

"One slice of warm apple pie along with one scoop of vanilla ice cream," Molly announced, having asked earlier what she could get Shae to eat. The white porcelain dish was set gently on the table in front of her. "Can I get you a nice tall glass of milk to go with that? Maybe a coffee?"

"I'd love a hot cup of tea, please." Shae had found that drinking English style tea reduced her stress level by half. She'd read quite a lot of different reports on how certain beverages could alter the way a person dealt with stress in their life. Seeing as she had an abundance of it, she'd given the theory a try by switching from coffee to tea. It had successfully worked in her daily life. "Thank you, Molly."

The waitress had been about to say something to Shae when the bell above the door jingled, alerting everyone to another newcomer. In this case, a father and son.

Shae was glad she hadn't taken a bite of her apple pie. She wasn't so sure she would have been able to swallow it around the knot that had formed in her throat.

As she lived and breathed, it was none other than Jace Kendall.

He'd changed since the last time she saw him, somehow managing to become even more strikingly attractive. She couldn't help but rake her eyes down him to prove to herself that he was real. His shoulders had gained considerable width, inches had been added to his over six-foot height, and he still had that charming, crooked grin that could melt a girl's heart like ice on a hot summer's day.

Yet all she experienced upon setting her gaze on his gorgeous features was guilt.

She'd heard that two of his brothers—Noah and Lance—had returned home from their time in the service. Their combined chosen path had been the Marine Corps, if she wasn't mistaken. Her mother had mentioned that Jace wasn't due back to Blyth Lake until the end of the year, which was probably why seeing him was such a blow to the serenity she'd been trying to marshal.

Her original plan had called for her to be out of Blyth Lake before he returned.

It wasn't personal. She was here for a purpose.

Shae was grateful that the diners had averted Jace's attention with their overzealous reception. He hadn't glanced her way, so he didn't even know that she was there. The distraction gave her time to slip out of the booth and head to the restroom, though her path took her right past the small group of greeters. No one noticed, and it wasn't long before she was behind a locked door and leaning over the sink to give her time to regain her composure.

"Why me?" Shae whispered to herself, hanging her head a little lower as she fought off the dancing lights. "I just needed a few weeks, Emma. Was that too much to ask? He will prove to be nothing but a distraction."

Shae didn't believe for a second that her baby sister was alive. She never had, regardless that her parents had proposed that scenario a time or two over the years. It had been easy for her to slip into a one-sided conversation, believing that Emma's spirit was somewhere out there watching over all of them.

Then there were times when Shae's unanswered requests made her question her own sanity. Talking with ghosts was crazy, wasn't it?

One of the saving graces about returning to her childhood home was knowing Jace Kendall wouldn't be in town. Shae understood that it wasn't fair to him, but he was a trigger of guilt that she couldn't deal with right now. She calculated her chances of just paying her tab and leaving without being noticed.

After all, he'd been the reason she'd taken the car the night Emma disappeared. Given her profession, she understood that the *what-if* game wasn't healthy to her mental state. She just couldn't prevent the perpetual question from rising to the surface once again—would Emma still be alive if Shae hadn't been with Jace Kendall that fateful night?

No one would ever know. Not unless Shae got the opportunity to personally ask Emma's killer.

CHAPTER FOUR

S HE STILL WORE the same perfume, not that he was surprised.

Jace didn't have to turn his head to know that Shae Irwin was the woman who had just slipped past everyone gathered to greet him. He did his best to maintain his focus on the old friends and acquaintances who embraced him rather than observe her as she made her way to the restroom. These people had been a part of his upbringing, and he wouldn't disregard their warm welcomes. Nor would he put Shae on the spot in front of them.

He couldn't say her brush-off didn't hurt, though. They'd been good friends in high school, and at one point he thought their friendship could be much more. Unfortunately, he'd caught mono in the last semester of his senior year. He'd missed out on all of the best parties, his senior prom, and he'd even had to delay his ship date to Marine Corps boot camp…which happened to be a couple days after Emma had gone missing.

Jace couldn't judge Shae on her lack of sociability. He'd been somewhat caught up on the events of the last few months, but one thing was clear—Emma Irwin's disappearance was once again front and center here in Blyth Lake. He could only imagine that the pain of losing a sister never really went away. He honestly couldn't fathom how he would deal with such a loss if anything suspicious were to happen to any of his siblings.

He had to believe that Shae understood he was there for her should she want to talk, a shoulder to cry on, or just someone to sit with for company in her hour of need. After all, he believed old friendships remained even through the longest of years. He'd given her space and would continue to do so for as long as she wanted to remain at a distance. Maybe an appropriate time would come when they could get caught up with one another's lives, because that was what friends did. There was always hope when even just one of them kept the faith.

"Harlan, I want to thank you for everything you did regarding the Stoll property." Jace shook his head, still in somewhat disbelief over the announcement his father had made this afternoon. "It's hard to believe such a beautiful house and those pristine sixteen acres of rolling pastures are now mine. It's…hell, I don't think there are words enough to describe what I feel right now."

Gus Kendall rested a hand on Jace's shoulder in understanding.

His father's support meant everything. As for his mother's final wish, well, that had been to have her children home and raising their own families in their hometown of Blyth Lake. What Jace and his siblings hadn't been made aware of was that she made that possible with an inheritance she'd saved for a special occasion. It was to be used when her sons and daughter returned from their duties to their country.

"It was my pleasure," Harlan replied in kind. He didn't mention being questioned by the police regarding those real estate transactions. "You Kendall kids might have raised hell back in the day, but it'll be nice to have a younger generation around to see to it this town survives with this economy. We've managed to keep Main Street a viable business community thus far. It didn't happen by itself, though. It takes invested people who want this town to thrive."

"Here, here." Chester raised his glass of water in the air while others repeated his sentiment. "Welcome home, Jace."

He and his dad settled at one of the tables, seeing as all the booths were taken. It didn't take a rocket scientist to figure out where Shae had been seated. A lone slice of Molly's apple pie with a scoop of melting hand-churned ice cream had been left in the back booth. Molly was currently setting down a coffee cup, but it could have been tea. A small square tab hung from a string connected to a nondescript white bag which accompanied the mug.

Where was she? He was beginning to wonder if she was alright.

Jace glanced toward the restrooms, but she had yet to make a return appearance.

"Brynn mentioned the other day that Shae was coming into town for an indefinite period of time." Gus had pulled out his reading glasses and was looking over the menu, even though he always got the meatloaf special. The menu had only changed once in the past forty years, and that was when the diner had been handed down from mother to daughter. People still referred to the old menu, though. It was hard to break long-standing traditions. Gus' order was always the exact same. That was, unless it was lunch. Then he preferred a club sandwich and steak fries. Jace imagined they would be able to determine Gus' age one day by cutting him in half and counting the rings in his arteries. "She's staying in that studio apartment above the Cavern. You know the one, in case you're interested."

Jace leaned back to give Molly room after giving his father a side-eye shot of irritation. He hadn't meant to be obvious in searching for Shae, but there was also nothing wrong with him wanting to say hi to an old friend.

Molly set down two porcelain coffee mugs, minus the saucers, and began pouring the steaming hot beverage he'd come to rely on during those long deployments overseas. Good coffee was a gift from heaven, no matter where one went. Her next statement made him realize the same thing about small towns. One was no different than the other.

"Shae is meeting with Detective Kendrick tomorrow afternoon around two or three o'clock." Molly didn't bother to pull out the waitress pad stored in the front of her apron. Jace must not have sold his indifference to her statement very well. She shrugged her skepticism and smiled at his obvious failure. "That sharp looking detective was in here just the other day, talking on his smartphone. He shouldn't carry on private conversations in public if he doesn't want the town to know all his business."

"Molly, I think I'll have the meatloaf special. Brown gravy over those mashed potatoes and meat." Gus leaned forward and slid the menu back into its slot in the metal prong holder behind the salt and pepper. "And save me a slice of that peach pie, if the last piece hasn't already been claimed. I don't know what Cassie added to that recipe, but it sure is good."

"It's all yours, Gus." Molly waited for Jace to order, but he was still mulling over the fact that the state police detective didn't have the good sense to talk business in the privacy of his own damned vehicle. Unless he wanted the residents to know who he was meeting, along with the where and when. "Jace? What can I get you?"

"I'll have the pulled pork sandwich with steak fries, thanks."

"I'll have to barbeque those steaks up tomorrow." Gus shook his head at the jumbled homecoming Jace had received today. He thought it was perfect. After all, he'd been surrounded by family. That's all one could ask for after having been gone for so long. "It shouldn't take too long to get my tank filled up over at the gas station. I hope they fix the treads on the regulator after those campers hosed it up. How hard is it to ask someone if you don't know what the hell you're doing? I'll let the others know to be at the house at eighteen hundred hours."

"You won't hear me complaining about anything," Jace said, fully comprehending how lucky he was after spending the last couple of hours at his new home. He figured if the barbecue had taken place the way his dad had wanted, the tour of the Stoll property wouldn't have occurred until the next morning. "Ed and Harriett Stoll kept that farmhouse in pretty good shape. Even the kitchen appliances had been bought brand new to further a quick sale. They are still under the manufacturer's warranty."

Sixteen acres of picturesque farmland, a couple of good-sized ponds, and a large-sized corral built from heavy timbers was the icing on the cake of finally coming home to stay.

And it was all his. It was a gift that he would always cherish, and one that would always remind him of how precious family truly was in the grand scheme of things.

"You'll have to call those TMO people and see if they can schedule a delivery of your furniture from the port in the next few days." TMO was the Traffic Management Office. They moved military personnel from one duty station to the next and then home after your service was completed. "Until then, you can stay in your old room back at the homestead. It'll be nice to have someone staying at the house for a while."

Jace had always taken advantage of the bachelor's quarters on base, never seeing the reason to own a home when he was rarely in country. He spent the vast majority of his time deployed or TAD. TAD stood for Temporary Additional Duty.

He liked to stay busy, taking every assignment he could muster. He never even thought about what he'd do when he came home until his older brother, Mitch, mentioned that Noah had bought the Yoder place. Tack on Lance's purchase of the Fetter farm, and it had been a foregone assumption on Jace's part that they were trying to outdo one another.

Now that Jace had all the facts, it all made more sense. Unfortunately, he had to keep this amazing gift under wraps so as not to spoil the surprise for either Gwen or Mitch. It was a wonder Lance had been able to keep his mouth shut, given that the average time for him to totally break like a dried-up branch at the end of autumn was about a half-second. When the secret was too good or he was pushed hard enough, he usually wasn't able to help himself.

It was good to know that his baby brother had finally grown into a mature man.

"...barn you'll have to replace. Maybe you could get one of those new all steel pole barns."

Gus cautiously took a drink from his freshly topped off coffee, thankfully giving Jace time to catch up on the conversation. He'd let his mind wander over all the things he wanted to do to his new place. It was like having Christmas in August. It was an exciting time that he wouldn't allow to be overshadowed by what had happened over at Noah and Lance's properties.

His train of thought took a header off the trestle the same moment Shae Irwin walked out of the restroom, her dark gaze immediately catching his.

Time stalled for a brief moment.

Jace couldn't comprehend what the difference was between high school and now. Shae had always been a cute girl, but the woman heading his way was strikingly beautiful...almost hauntingly so. Her ethereal presence stole every ounce of air from his lungs. He was struck dumb and unable to break her gaze. He found himself wondering how long it had been since a smile had graced those pink lips of hers?

"Mr. Kendall and Jace, it's good to see you once again." Shae dropped his look and focused on Gus as she stood in front of their table. "I wasn't able to make it back to town for Mrs. Kendall's funeral. I'm truly sorry for your family's loss."

"Thank you, dear," Gus replied kindly, setting his coffee cup on the table. Jace noticed that the level of conversation in the diner had fallen somewhat silent. "It was a beautiful service, and we miss her every day. I'm sorry to see that Emma's disappearance is front page news again. One would think that the newspapers would be more circumspect of the families involved. I can only imagine the grief your family has been through over the years. To have it all brought back up and prolonged is an atrocity. Inappropriate, at the very least."

"Thank you, Mr. Kendall." It seemed as if Shae had to drag her gaze from Gus to Jace. He also noted that she crossed her arms as she politely addressed him…almost too politely, in retrospect. "Jace, welcome home. Brynn mentioned that you, your brothers, and your sister were all coming home at different times this year."

"I arrived in town today," Jace shared, leaning back in his chair. It was evident he made her uncomfortable, and yet he had no idea why. "How long are you home for, Shae?"

Home was a relative word for her, wasn't it? Her parents no longer lived here, and according to what he'd heard the last time he'd been in town, Shae was some type of psychologist or psychiatrist at a prestigious hospital somewhere in Michigan. The only thing that tied her to Blyth Lake were childhood memories and the fact that her sister's body had never been found.

"Shae, please. I'm not here professionally," Shae replied, peeking over at her booth. Jace followed her line of vision to find that the vanilla ice cream had pretty much melted over what had to be an ice-cold slice of apple pie. "I'm not sure about the length of my visit quite yet. I'm meeting with Detective Kendrick tomorrow, and I thought maybe revisiting the old house and some of our old hangouts might jog my memory of some detail that could help."

Jace wanted to offer the sound advice of not torturing herself over something she couldn't change, but it was doubtful she'd listen to him. He'd been in far too many horrific situations that he would have given anything to change. Each individual had to come to some understanding on their own that one couldn't change the past. She would never succeed in doing so.

"Well, if you need anything, you must stop by the house and let me know." Gus gestured toward Jace with a pointed finger. "You two went to school together, didn't you?"

"Be careful," Molly warned Gus, saving Shae from responding. The waitress set the two meals on the table. "Your plate is hot, Gus."

The tension in Shae's shoulders faded somewhat as she recognized the out offered to her by Molly. It wasn't that Gus' question was difficult to answer, but it led into a longer conversation that Shae apparently didn't want to have at the moment…or if ever, for that matter.

Jace would have questioned if he'd done something in the past to upset her that he wasn't aware of, but the reason was glaringly obvious—the Kendalls had reinitiated the investigation into her sister's disappearance. Technically, Noah was to blame. But Shae was acting like Jace had the plague.

"I'll let you two enjoy your dinner." Shae lifted a half-raised hand in farewell. "It was good to see you both."

Now that was a flat out lie if he ever heard one. Jace couldn't take his gaze off her as she slid in the booth and pushed away her uneaten slice of pie. Instead, she reached into her purse and pulled out her phone as she settled back against the seat.

"She's been away for a long time." Gus used the edge of his fork to cut into the thick slice of meatloaf. His insight told Jace that his dad hadn't missed a thing. "Give her a few days to get reacquainted with the everyone, and she won't be so wary of those who really care about her."

Jace wasn't so sure about that, given that Shae had her phone pressed against her ear and was talking to someone in a hushed tone. She used to be good friends with Stephanie Green and Andrea Cox back in the day, but those two hadn't lived in the area in quite some time. Besides Brynn and Julie—who had been Emma's closest friends—who would be there for Shae when she needed advice or comfort?

She was an adult and more than capable of taking care of herself. He imagined that she liked it that way.

Gus switched topics and started talking about the renovations to the barn he'd mentioned earlier. Jace did his best to listen and concentrate on the pulled pork in front of him. It was his first day back home, and he had best cherish every second of it. He grimaced when the vibration of his cell phone cut into his effort to do just that.

"Sorry, Dad," Jace mumbled, leaning back in his chair so that he could take the cell phone out of the front pocket of his jeans. The display read a number he wasn't familiar with, and he almost ignored the call. Something told him to answer. "Hello?"

"Jace Kendall? This is Detective Kendrick. I'm investigating the murder of Whitney Bell, as well as the disappearance of several young girls dating back over a twelve-year period."

"I'm aware of who you are, Detective." Jace's reply caught his dad's attention, as well as every other diner in the place…including Shae Irwin, who was looking over his way while seeming to pause the conversation on her own phone.

Well, this couldn't be good. "What can I do for you?"

"I know this is an odd request, but I'd like to stop by tomorrow morning with a forensics team and search the premises of your newly acquired property. I'm sure I don't need to explain to you the reason why, but…"

Detective Kendrick went into more detail as to why he was making such an appeal, even though he could have easily obtained a warrant to carry out such a task after linking the most recent discoveries to the other properties his father had purchased. Jace understood the detective's quandary at not wanting to upset any more of the locals, yet needing some type of lead that would end the threat of terror that had seized this town. So far, two houses that were bought by Gus Kendall had been tied to a serial killer. It wasn't a stretch to believe that the other three properties could contain some type of evidence, as well.

Unfortunately, this type of request could easily be misconstrued by the other residents. Rumors were bound to fly and stir up the inevitable hornet's nest.

"I'll be there," Jace replied, making sure he didn't convey too many details to those who were hanging onto his every word. "Goodnight, Detective."

"What was that about?" Gus asked warily, setting down his utensils before wiping his mouth with a napkin. His concern for all of his children was written across his face.

"Just like Shae, I'm meeting with Detective Kendrick tomorrow." Jace made eye contact with his father, who understood there was more to the story. He took the hint, though, that it wasn't something he wanted to share with everyone in their proximity. "It's routine background questions. Nothing more."

Jace purposefully avoided Shae's questioning stare from across the diner. All would be made clear with time. He concentrated on his sandwich platter and began talking to his dad about the changes he'd like to make to the barn. He didn't much care for the pole barn idea. Eventually, everyone went back to their meals and private conversations.

It was a good thing Noah and Lance hadn't joined them for dinner. Jace might very well have been arrested for a murder, though it would have been his own kin. He'd waited twelve long years to come home for good, and now his ass was being dragged into an old murder investigation.

What the hell had his brothers gotten him into?

CHAPTER FIVE

S HAE REPEATEDLY DIPPED her Lipton's teabag into the hot water she'd warmed up in the microwave a moment before she walked to the window. It was a little after seven o'clock in the morning, but she hadn't been able to sleep past five. Her recent bout of insomnia had become an unpleasant habit. She couldn't legally write herself a prescription for sleep medication. It was just as well. She'd long ago accepted that no drug could kill the root of her problem.

She leaned against the windowsill as she looked down on Main Street. A lone vehicle drove through town, but she didn't recognize the driver. There were quite a few new faces she could add to her catalog she classified as locals. The streets were quiet on this Saturday morning, though that was bound to change as the time grew near for her meeting with Detective Kendrick.

Saturday afternoons were usually busy here in town. Those who commuted to the city during the week would be home and catching up on their projects and chores.

She and Detective Kendrick had decided days ago that they should have their talk somewhere private. The studio apartment she was staying at above the bar would provide a venue of discretion. It would serve its purpose without adding too much intrigue for the residents of Blyth Lake to blather on about. It wasn't like the authorities had anything to tell her that she didn't already know. This upcoming meeting was what her fellow colleagues referred to as a basal foray. Shae understood it would amount to nothing more than an initial reconnaissance mission into hostile territory.

Shae blew on the contents of the steaming cup before tentatively testing the temperature of the darkening liquid. Still too hot to drink, although it was time to remove the blend. Morning tea was meant to be stimulating, not bold.

The movement of yet another vehicle driving down Main Street caught her attention. This time, the car didn't sail past the parking lot of the Cavern, but instead turned in and parked. It was then that she could make out the individual behind the wheel. What was Brynn doing at the bar so early?

Shae pushed off the ledge of the window, figuring she'd go downstairs and keep Brynn company rather than waiting for the eventual knock at the door. The two of them hadn't had a chance to talk at length. Other than Brynn handing Shae a key over for the apartment last night while mixing a cocktail, they might have exchanged a handful of words since her arrival.

She didn't bother to lock the door behind her, carefully walking down the inner staircase rather than using the private exit that led to the parking lot outside. She was very confident in the fact that she wouldn't spill a drop of her tea. Grace was one of her qualities, though she was quite short in many others.

"Brynn?" Shae searched the bar area, but didn't see the honey blonde owner. A few muttered curse words drifted back from the short hallway that led to the restrooms and Brynn's office, announcing her whereabouts. "Is everything okay back there? You're here rather early."

"Oh, I can't find my damn purse," Brynn replied, rolling the chair away from her desk. She glanced underneath with a frown. "I couldn't find it at the house, so I thought I'd left it here last night."

"Red?" Shae asked, pointing to the filing cabinet in the corner where a small clutch had been set on the top.

"Thank you!" Brynn exclaimed, throwing her hands up in victory. She quickly snatched it up before advancing to the door. "Are you heading over to Jace's new house?"

She must have misunderstood Brynn, because there was no valid reason why Shae would visit Jace. Not for any reason she could determine, anyway. Their friendship had faded long ago. For all intents and purposes, they were complete strangers. Last night proved to her that she had warped feelings about the man. *No, it was better to stay away.*

"Um, no, I hadn't planned to," Shae answered, taking a sip of her tea to cover up her unease.

The sweetness from the teaspoon of sugar she'd put into the cup caused her system to flush with endorphins. At least, that was the reason she attributed for the slight tremor of her fingers and not the mere mention of his name. She had counseled compulsive eaters who were in fact slowly killing themselves with high sugar diets. Her rationalization was just another introspective path to avoid yet another bout of guilt.

She should have downed the contents of her cup sooner.

Often, working as a psychiatrist made dealing with her feelings more complex. Her thoughts became tangled up with ethical dilemmas and ethereal motives rather than simple solutions.

"I was up early and happened to see you pull into the parking lot. I'm thinking of going to see Julie this morning. I haven't talked to her in quite some time."

"I'm warning you now, she's been dating Billy Stanton. What an ass." Brynn shook her head in disappointment. Shae's stomach revolted upon hearing the man's name. The tea didn't taste as good coming back up. "I've had several conversations with Julie, but she won't listen to me."

"I didn't know that." Shae could hear Billy's villainous words about how he'd only danced with Emma that fateful night out of pity, not because he felt anything for her. The sharp slice of anger was as fresh today as it had been then. "It might be best I put off that reunion, then."

"Are you sure you don't want to drive out to Jace's new property with me? Detective Kendrick said he'd be there with a forensics team around eight o'clock." Brynn glanced at the black and white clock hanging on the side wall of her office. "We can ride together since I have to be back here at ten thirty anyway. I just need to make a quick stop at the bakery for their house coffee blend and a dozen donuts. Who knows how long the search will take? Those forensics lab guys are pretty thorough."

It was as if Shae were trying to take part in a discussion where she only heard one side of the conversation. Her conflicting emotions were quickly becoming muffled inside her head.

"Brynn, why is Detective Kendrick having a forensics team search Jace's property?"

She and the detective had engaged in long conversations about the Kendalls involvement in Sophia Morton's murder, as well as Emma's disappearance. She agreed with him that it was entirely circumstantial, and there was nothing of substance to be gained from pursuing that line of investigation further. These crimes were committed over a decade ago, and the finding of Sophia's body had provided closure to her family. Well, some small measure of closure.

As for Lance subsequently discovering pictures of the victims in his basement, one could only assume the previous homeowner—Arthur Fetter—had something to do with the missing girls or that the pictures were a plant to skew the investigation. Either one of those two possibilities had some teeth. Or maybe someone connected with the Fetters hid them at the house at some point over the years. Seeing as he was well into his eighties and his estranged children weren't anywhere around Blyth Lake at the time of Emma's disappearance, that left the police with nothing to follow up on.

Brynn telling Shae the latest update had her second guessing her original stance.

Were the Kendalls somehow involved?

"You didn't know?" Brynn asked, somewhat startled by that fact. "I'm so sorry, Shae. Jace mentioned last night that he ran into you at the diner. I assumed you were there when Detective Kendrick called and asked to search his property, given what happened to Noah and Lance when they took possession of their homes. I can follow the detective's logic if the killer is truly trying to implicate the family's involvement. Better to nip whatever thorny flower is planted than to stumble on it and draw blood."

Shae wasn't sure she should be relieved that there wasn't more to Detective Kendrick's reasoning in searching Jace's house or she should be pissed at Jace for not informing her as a courtesy. It wasn't as if he owed her anything, but she had been sitting in the diner when he got the call. Why would he keep it from her?

Shae wasn't usually the spontaneous type, but she quickly made the decision to take Brynn up on her offer.

"I wasn't aware of the search, but you know what? I think I will join you, after all." Shae glanced down at the shorts and t-shirt she'd thrown on this morning. She'd planned on getting a shower and changing before meeting with Detective Kendrick, and that was still the plan…just accelerated a bit. "What house did Jace buy? I need to change and take care of a few things first, but I can meet you out there."

"I can see we're going to have to sit down to catch you up on the comings and goings in Blyth Lake. The Kendall boys didn't buy those houses." Brynn raised her right eyebrow, stressing another fact that Shae hadn't been made aware of in the twelve hours she'd been in town. "Mary and Gus bought each of the boys and Gwen houses as their homecoming gifts. It was Mary's dying wish that each of them would raise their families here. Noah now owns the old Yoder farm and Lance lives out at the Fetters' farm. Jace was given the former Stoll horse ranch west of town. He only found out yesterday."

Shae had assumed that Noah and Lance had purchased their new homes when they'd gotten to town, but now she understood why Kendrick dismissed their connection. That bit of knowledge leaned her toward believing the detective wanted access to the property not because of Jace, but because of who may have had access to the houses prior to the boys' arrival back in town.

"That was very generous of Mary and Gus to do that for their children," Shae said with utmost sincerity. She'd always liked the older couple who had played cards with her parents once a week. She didn't think they had the kind of money needed to buy five commercial properties, but people around here kept their prosperity, or lack thereof, to themselves. That was, with the exception of the Stantons. They made it their business to spread their affluence throughout the entire county. "You don't think Jace will mind me showing up out of the blue, do you?"

"Of course not." Brynn wiggled her fingers for Shae to get a move on. "Jace wants to help as much as he can. He's a friend of your family. Now go. I'll run over to the bakery and then meet you out at his place."

Shae backed out of Brynn's office and then walked around the corner behind the small stage she'd installed for the live bands to play on during the weekend. Her cup of tea was still fairly full, so she carefully made her way upstairs. She locked the door behind her, knowing she'd take the outer exit to the parking lot below when it was time to leave.

She forced herself to walk to the small kitchen instead of hurrying over to her suitcase, which remained full of her clothes. Unpacking was something she'd not managed to find time for just yet. She needed every minute to get her thoughts in order. Emptying the contents of her cup down the drain and throwing away the used tea bag, she had to wonder if she wasn't setting herself up for disappointment getting personally involved following up on another useless lead.

All she'd ever wanted to do was find out the truth about what happened to her sister. It logically followed that now might be that time given Sophia's body being discovered a few months ago to Whitney being brutally murdered. It meant Shae might finally get her wish—a chance to get justice for Emma.

The most compelling and disturbing question remained— would the individual responsible be a total stranger or would it be someone she'd grown up with throughout her childhood in Blyth Lake?

CHAPTER SIX

J ACE DRAGGED HIS gaze from the front door of his house to the old barn located immediately to the south. Noah, Reese, Lance, and Brynn did the same. It was like watching a massive grownup game of hide and seek or an action flick with an epic chase scene between the good guys and the insane douchebags who had the home turf advantage, keeping themselves three blocks ahead of the pack of the pursuing patrol cars.

Detective Kendrick had arrived with two complete forensics teams—a unit to search inside the house and larger crew to explore the surrounding land. They even had ground penetrating radar, which the technician said was only capable of reaching a depth of six feet down unless the soil was loosely packed.

The measly ten minutes since their arrival felt more like hours already. Herds of lab nerds in white coats and purple gloves were setting up a small cover tent with several folding tables to support their equipment, maps, and grid markers. Buckets with tiny plastic flags, numbered cones, and evidence bags were readied just in case something was discovered. It was a good thing Brynn picked up a dozen donuts and coffee. Half of the sugar-inducing coma food was already gone, leaving them to subsist on caffeine.

"What is it that they're searching for exactly?" Brynn asked after she'd practically chewed off the end of her straw. Her comment had an edge to it, as if to say that she would rather watch golf on television than spend one more minute looking at these techies polish their expensive toys. How she could drink soda at this hour of the morning was beyond him. "I mean, are they looking for more mementos the killer left behind like a trail of breadcrumbs? Or do they think…"

Brynn's voice trailed off before she said Emma's name. She wasn't the only one to believe that was why Kendrick wanted to bring a team out to a home that had been listed by the same realtor who had sold the other properties to the Kendall family. The chances that only the first two properties were the ones to contain evidence related to the same twelve-year old investigation were remote. Kendrick must have suspected that the killer was trying to involve the Kendalls or felt the need to taunt the police while steering the investigation in some random direction.

The detective seemed like an upstanding officer. He had a by-the-book mentality and followed the letter of the law, cataloging information and putting the check in the crime scene investigation box exactly per the Ohio State Police's SOP playbook. There was no doubting the man preferred city life, but he was slowly learning the time-honored traditions of a small town in Midwest America. He'd learned the hard way that he gained more from honey than vinegar. A little bit of common courtesy went a long way in getting the locals to open up and volunteer information.

"Maybe I shouldn't have told Shae that she could join us. This isn't exactly a spectator's sport."

Jace did a double take, but it was too late to ask Brynn why she would have extended such an invitation as he looked down his driveway. The sound of gravel crunching underneath the tires of a vehicle would have drowned out his words anyway.

Son of a bitch.

What had Brynn been thinking? She all but said herself there was a chance Emma's body might be recovered today. It certainly wasn't out of the realm of possibility, which put Shae in an uncomfortable position. He'd witnessed the vulnerability in her eyes when his dad had inadvertently brought up Emma in conversation last night. It was part of the reason he'd held back from telling her about Kendrick's call to begin with.

Jace hopped down from the back of his brother's truck, needing a moment with Shae in private. Noah and Lance had parked their F150s side by side, dropping the tailgates so they all had a place to sit while monitoring the progress of today's events. Their father had a delivery to make this morning, so he'd be joining them later. As for Jace, he sure as hell wasn't going to allow this search to take place on his property without being here to oversee the exploration.

"Good morning." Jace had opened Shae's car door before she'd turned off the engine. She didn't seem at all to mind the annoying ding telling her she forgot to take her car keys out of the ignition as she exited the vehicle. "Shae, I want you to know I didn't keep this from you because I thought the police would find anything here. I didn't want you to get your hopes up for—"

"Jace, in case you didn't notice after all these years, I'm a grown woman capable of managing my own affairs." It was hard to see what she was thinking from the oversized brown sunglasses she wore to cover her eyes, but she definitely got her point across. She wasn't being condescending in any way. She was merely pointing out that she could handle whatever the authorities might find today. "I know you thought you were doing me a favor, but I don't need you to act as if you are some kind of shining knight saving the damsel in distress. I'm neither a damsel nor distressed."

Jace was left to close her car door as she strolled forward toward the others making sure to stay out of OSP Forensics

Team's way, nodding to the collection of family members as she took a few tentative steps toward the house. Detective Kendrick had been watching the exchange from his position at the front porch, though he stayed where he was to finish speaking with one of the forensics techs who was holding some type of device in his hand that he'd waved over the porch and front outside wall of the house.

The home had one of those wraparound porches that only covered three sides. It didn't extend to the back of the house, truly a shame considering the potential for an open deck, but those views were plentiful from the scenic walkout seating area the Stolls had installed a few years ago. One didn't have to stretch their imagination too hard to see the exquisiteness now betrayed by all the overgrown weeds coming up through the limestone pad which lay between the house and the barn.

A little preventative maintenance for the next few weeks and a half an hour with a skid loader spreading a fresh load of crushed limestone mixed with broken oyster shells and sand was all that was needed to restore its beauty. People from the Midwest called the mixture limestone cement, which set hard enough to support heavy farm equipment. The owner just needed to keep the weeds from taking root. Jace was behind the power curve in this case, but all would be attended to once he had a green light from the detective.

"Shae." Jace wasn't sure she'd stop to hear what he had to say, but she surprised him by walking back to her car. He'd already closed the door, silencing the irritating noise. An awkward silence hung in the air. "I'm sorry. I should have told you. I should have been up front with you."

Shae parted her pink lips, the pretty color matching her lightweight blouse. She was wearing a pair of white pants that were most likely bleached denim jeans, but he didn't want to drop his eyes to find out if he was correct. She'd most likely take an obvious visual inspection the wrong way. It was just that he noticed she had a professional air about her that made it seem as if she were wearing some type of armor. He realized it must be the proficient demeanor she used when working with her patients at the hospital.

Maybe she was masking herself.

"Thank you." Shae slowly removed her sunglasses, revealing to him that stark vulnerability he'd been concerned with last night. Her dark brown eyes were surrounded with long lashes that did nothing to hide the concern about what was happening behind her. "I've spent almost twelve years waiting for Emma to be found. I want this over with. I want results. I want her to find peace, and I want to be able to live my life without believing every phone call is going to be *the one*."

Jace fought back the urge to take her in his arms and tell her that everything would be alright, but that might prove to be a fatal mistake. He'd never had the chance to tell her that before, or be by her side during those initial days after Emma's disappearance. Hell, the night Emma had been taken, he'd been at a small party a town over where he'd spent the night instead of driving home. Shae had even shown up, but she'd left after a couple of hours without saying a word to him.

The first of many search parties had been conducted the following day that his younger brothers had taken part in, but Jace hadn't made it back to town until later that afternoon. His mother told him that the local and state police had things covered, and the townsfolk were lining up to show their support for the Irwins. His job was to pack up his room and get ready to catch the bus to MEPS in Cleveland. They would fly him out for boot camp at Parris Island, South Carolina because that was what was expected of him.

"Let's go grab you a coffee and then we'll take a walk. Trust me, sitting here watching the lab coats search every inch of this place for more than ten minutes is like watching paint dry." Jace could see her hesitation, but she conceded when she realized the detective had disappeared into the house. It couldn't have been hard for her to distinguish who was in charge. "I won't be able to show you the inside quite yet, but I can give you a tour of the property."

Shae fell into step by his side as they made their way over to where everyone was trying to act casual about watching his and Shae's every move. Noah and Lance had their boots on the ground to offer their greetings, while Reese appeared somewhat nervous. Brynn was still chewing on her straw and watching the comings and goings from the house behind them.

"Shae, it's been a long time." Noah moved over a step when Reese indicated she wanted down from the bed of his truck. "This is Reese Woodward."

"I'm truly sorry we're meeting under these conditions," Reese replied softly, an honesty in her voice that reminded Jace she was having a hard time with today's events, as well. She waved her hand in helplessness toward the chaos. "I feel like this is somehow partly my fault. I didn't mean to drag you and your family through—"

Shae stepped forward and hugged Reese, her kind gesture saying she didn't blame anyone for the turmoil over the past few months. These two women had lost family members to who the police assumed was one insanely sick and twisted individual. It was a connection they would have for the rest of their lives.

"Emma mentioned Sophia a few times after they attended summer camp together," Shae said after having stepped back, giving Noah room to rest his hand on Reese's lower back. She leaned into him, seeking his support. "I wasn't home much that summer as I was getting ready for college and hanging out with my friends, but I do remember her saying how nice Sophia was and that she helped Emma learn how to swim. I'm sorry that you had to find your cousin the way you did."

Which was exactly why Jace hadn't wanted Shae to know about today's search. What if Emma was buried on this land? What if Harlan Whitmore had something to do with the murders? Or Miles Schaeffer, for that matter? A ton of people had access to these old properties that had been on the market for some time before becoming part of this case. Detective Kendrick wasn't searching Jace's house because he had nothing better to do. He clearly believed there was a motive behind the Kendall connection and that the killer had an axe to grind with the family.

It looked as if their walk was going to have to wait. Everyone began talking and catching up with their past, especially the vital incidents over this past summer. Jace noticed that Shae declined the coffee, holding onto her sunglasses as if they would give her strength to see this day through. It wasn't his place to ask if she'd eaten breakfast, but he couldn't help but wonder if she was taking care of herself.

He found himself studying her, noticing some of her mannerisms hadn't changed since she was in high school. She still tilted her head slightly to the right when listening to someone speak, just like she used to do when a teacher was giving a lecture. It was an endearing quality, though every now and then he noticed her gaze flick to the left where a forensics team was entering and exiting the barn. She wasn't missing a thing.

A random thought about homeowner's insurance crossed his mind. Would there be a payout if the rotted wood on the porch collapsed on state employees?

"Jace? I think I'd like that tour now."

He ignored the questioning looks he received from his brothers, pushing off Lance's truck without reaching for what was left of his coffee. It was sure to be cold now, anyway.

The warm sun was becoming hotter as the morning wore on, bringing with it a bit of humidity. Jace didn't mind it though, considering September was only a couple of days away. The fall season would be here in a blink of an eye, bringing with it Halloween and Thanksgiving.

He would love to have the barn renovated before the first snowfall arrived, but he figured that all depended on what the police found in their search today. He could arrange for the contractor to put up the new siding and complete the insulation of the structure, but he would have to strip the old rotting boards that needed to come out and provide a solid frame prior to the siding going up.

"Weren't you into horseback riding when you were younger?" Shae asked, slipping her sunglasses back on as they walked around the barn.

"I was, unlike my brothers. Gwen and I used to go riding out on the horse farm at the north edge of town. You remember the one, up near the lake." Jace almost warned her to be careful of splinters as she reached for the corral fence, but she pulled her hand away upon seeing that the wood wasn't in the best of shape. "The Happel Horse Farm."

"Will you take riding back up now that you have your own place?"

"For sure," Jace replied, continuing on the footpath once inside the paddock.

The trail had been worn into the ground over the years by dozens of Percheron draft horses. The Stolls had raised working animals, not riding horses, although the Percheron could technically be ridden. Jace was more partial to American quarter horses or thoroughbreds. The path they were on led to the edge of a tree line he'd yet to have a chance to explore.

"Fixing up the barn and buying a couple of horses will give me something to work on while I figure out what I want to do with my life."

"You have no idea?" Shae asked, sounding somewhat surprised. "You were always so…"

"If you say straight-laced and determined, I can't promise not to push you into that pond over there." Jace thought for a moment a smile might have graced her lips, but that was before she caught sight of a man and a woman over by one of the smaller ramshackle outbuildings off to the left of them. It was actually nothing more than an elaborate lean-to meant to protect feed and equipment from the elements. He couldn't blame her for her intermittent attention. "The service was all I knew. I'm not sure I'm properly prepared for civilian life."

"Take each day as it comes, and don't rush things."

Jace had temporarily forgotten she was a therapist of some sort. Actually, a doctor, if he remembered correctly. He fought the urge to stop this conversation in its tracks. He didn't want to be labeled or put into a box with every other veteran returning home from war. He'd been talking to her as an old friend, not a head-shrinker.

"What about you?" Jace asked, changing the subject so that he could know exactly who he was dealing with. She was no longer the pretty teenage girl who sat in front of him in math class. He'd learned early on to never underestimate any opponent. "I heard you were living somewhere up north in a big city."

Jace could still sense she wasn't quite comfortable in his presence. Again, he wondered if he'd said or done something to upset her. Was she reticent because he'd left for boot camp days after Emma's disappearance? He hadn't even been in town the night it happened.

"Lansing, Michigan." Shae sidestepped a small dip in the ground before he could warn her. She was wearing a pair of sandals with that pretty outfit of hers. He wasn't so sure they should have walked this far away from the house. "I work at one of the city hospitals as a psychiatrist. I've been there since I finished my residency."

"And your parents?" Jace veered to the left, figuring they could circle around the pond and head toward the back of the house. He wasn't quite sure why she agreed to this walk, anyway. Her responses were to the point, whereas she easily delved into his life. "Do they live in Lansing, too?"

"Yes, though they have a house in a nice suburb north of the city. They told me to stop by one of the Euchre game nights to say hi to everyone," Shae shared, though she effortlessly changed the subject with him once again. "You could always start your own card night, seeing as your younger brothers are back. I recall Lance getting caught in his freshman year for rounding a poker game in the lunchroom. I think it was Mr. Hughes who caught him dealing seconds. That must have put a dent in him practicing his mechanics to make a buck or two. I wouldn't play your brother at cards for all the tea in China."

"You're pretty good at that, you know." He'd caught her off guard. She pursed her lips so that the light gloss shimmered in the sunlight. He gently took hold of her upper arm, bringing her to a stop next to the small pond. They were around twenty yards from the backyard of the house, but he didn't want to have this discussion in front of strangers. "You're always bringing the conversation around to me so that you don't make a mistake and tell me what it is I've done to piss you off. Avoidance. Isn't that what they call it?"

Jace wasn't sure he should be grateful she didn't lie and try to get out of this confrontation with another dodge or become pissed off that she fell silent and nonverbally agreed with his statement. She even took a step back so that his fingers fell away from her arm.

"Shae, talk to me. Why are you upset with me? What have I done?"

CHAPTER SEVEN

SHAE STARED UP into Jace's blue eyes, his confusion more than evident. She truly wished she could wipe his look of perplexity away with a wave of her hand, but she would never lie. To dismiss his observation as trivial was a disservice to them both. She'd witnessed what dishonesty did to friendships, relationships, and marriages every day. He'd done nothing to deserve her anger or indignation.

And that was the problem.

How could she explain her unsubstantiated guilt over something he hadn't actually had any intent to commit?

Jace was absolutely right. She was an expert in diverting the conversations away from herself and redirecting the narrative. She'd done it since the day Emma disappeared. No one had ever called her out on it, though.

"I'm not exactly mad at you, Jace," Shae answered as honestly as she could, looking him directly in the eye so that he didn't doubt her response. She wasn't sure how she didn't stumble over her words. It was as if he could see right through her. "It's been tougher coming home than I thought it would be. Don't you find that to be true?"

There was a small flare of recognition in his features at the use of the word *home*. There was a part of her that would always recognize Blyth Lake as her home, but facing these childhood memories made her want to run away from her past and never return.

"You're doing it again. I want an answer."

Shae could see his confusion. It wasn't fair to him that she was harboring resentment for a contrived slight she had rationalized for her own purposes.

"Jace, I—"

"Ms. Irwin?"

Jace thinned his lips and crossed his arms at the interruption. His reaction told her that he wasn't letting this conversation go, but it did buy her some time.

"I'm Detective Kendrick. It's good to finally meet you."

"You, as well," Shae replied, holding out an arm. The detective had a firm handshake and didn't loosen his grip because she was a woman. She liked him already. "I'd heard that you were conducting a search of Jace's property. I hope you don't mind me being here."

"I'll be honest," Detective Kendrick shared as he looked around the area. "I'm grasping at straws. We've hit a dead end with the investigation."

"I'm aware that DNA evidence takes a few weeks." Shae was grateful she'd taken the time to apply her makeup and change her clothes. It made dealing with the unpleasantness of this situation bearable. "Is there a chance something will surface from Whitney's vehicle? Or her father's house?"

"Anything is possible, although I'm not holding out hope."

Detective Kendrick's tone told her all she needed to know about his conviction on the forensics of the case. This killer had gotten away with abducting and murdering girls for twelve years—maybe longer. He didn't get that way because he was careless or left physical evidence laying around to be found.

"I'd still like to meet with you this afternoon to go over some of the accounts the night your sister went missing to see if there are any discrepancies." The detective was already being called away by a technician near the barn. "If you'll excuse me for a moment."

Shae turned to continue walking toward the house where she and Jace had left the others when he caught her hand. The heat from his touch startled her, seeing as they'd both been walking in the sunshine. A part of her wanted to grab hold and soak in his warmth, but she instinctively pulled away.

"Are you upset with me because I went to boot camp that weekend? Shae, I'd already delayed my departure once due to illness. I couldn't—"

"It's not because of that."

"So there *is* a reason you have a hard time looking me in the eye every time we see each other."

Damn it. He'd gotten past her defenses. She scrambled for a way to give an answer without the outcome being one of embarrassment, but she came up empty. Where were all the techniques she'd learned in her profession over the years?

Shae figured sitting in the grass wasn't the smartest thing to do while wearing white pants, but she needed some support while baring her soul. Besides, the view of the small pond gave her something to look at instead of his piercing blue eyes.

"You wouldn't know that Emma and I argued the day she went missing."

Jace had yet to join her on the ground, but she could sense that he'd gone still. He most likely wasn't expecting her to open with that statement, but she only wanted to say this once.

"I argue with my brothers and sister all the time." Jace lowered his large frame down beside her, though he gave her some space. She didn't feel crowded, but instead secure. She'd analyze why later. "They know I love them just the same."

"Emma said she hated me." The slice of pain to Shae's heart

every time she replayed those words in her head never lost its power. "I could hear her and Mom arguing in the kitchen over who was getting the car that night. I was the oldest and had first right of refusal."

Shae drew her knees up to her chest, hoping to ease the throbbing ache in her chest.

"You were already in college." Jace raised one knee to rest his forearm on as he stared out over the water. She breathed a little easier knowing he wasn't observing her reactions. "I remember you and Stephanie complaining about not being allowed a car on campus your freshman year."

"It's amazing what teenagers believe to be the worst of times, isn't it?" Shae's protected view of the world had been ripped away in a brutal fashion. "Emma was upset I was using the car that night, because I'd had it the day before. It was her turn, according to her understanding of our deal with Mom."

"You're a psychologist, right? I don't need to tell you that playing the *what-if* game always produces nothing but losers. It's worse than gambling with my brother."

"I'm a psychiatrist, actually," Shae replied, honored by the success she'd achieved over the years. It was also the reason she'd come so far in accepting a life without her sister. That didn't mean she wasn't without emotional scars. "I try to stay away from the *what-if* game, but sometimes the draw is like the gravitational pull of the moon, shifting tides and the like."

"Wait. You came to the party that Nick threw for me that night."

Jace connected the dots, but there was still some left dangling in that maze of tangled emotions. She might as well pick up the pen for him and map it out.

"I came to see you. Don't you understand?" Shae let her words hang in the air, hoping she wouldn't have to explain herself further. They were too far from the water to see his reflection. She didn't have the courage to look at him. She'd seen enough pity on people's faces to last a lifetime. "I could have easily hitched a ride with Stephanie and let Emma have the car, but I was hoping to stay longer than that night."

There. The professional side of her was very proud of the way she'd faced her past. Now all she had to do was push past this awkwardness so that the issue was no longer between them. The knot in her chest loosened when he didn't comment, giving her a chance to explain the rest.

"It's not fair, but all I see is guilt when I look at you." Shae bravely snuck a glance his way, testing her theory. "I let a high school crush prevent me from being a good sister. She would have been safe. And yes, I know all the arguments about how unhealthy it is to place blame on myself. Trust me, I've had years of therapy to see the facts clearly. That doesn't mean it's always easy to take that advice. In fact, it makes it harder."

They sat in silence, though Shae found it comforting. Jace didn't try to make it better, nor did he say her emotions were unfounded, even though they were. She understood that in her mind, but emotionally it was a different story altogether. She glanced down when his hand found hers.

Distant sounds from the barn floated over the pond. The monotonous noise was disturbingly soothing. It meant that the police were actively looking for her sister's body.

"I understand Emma's gone." Shae wasn't sure why she said those words aloud. Jace had been keeping her company with no judgment as the minutes passed into hours. She wasn't even sure what time it was, but Brynn had left a while back. His fingers were still laced with hers in a comforting embrace. "I'd like to see her properly buried, though. I want to give her peace."

"Then that's what we'll strive to do." Jace unfolded his large frame, never letting go of her hand. He helped her off the ground, and that was when she realized he did have something to say. He'd just been waiting for the right moment. "I'm sorry you feel guilt when you look at me. I'd like to change that, if possible."

Shae wasn't sure what to say to his request, because it wasn't something she was expecting to hear. He might very well be asking her for the impossible. Unfortunately, she wasn't given the time to answer before chaos erupted.

"We've got company," Lance shouted, his voice carrying easily over the distance.

Jace led the way, still maintaining a hold on her hand. They quickly walked around the pond, bypassing the back of the house and a couple of the state's technicians. It wasn't until they'd rounded the corner that Lance's warning finally made sense.

Two media crews were driving up the hard-packed limestone driveway, leaving a trail of white dust in their wake.

"So much for keeping this quiet," Jace muttered, finally letting go of her hand as he forged forward to deal with what was sure to be the six o'clock news. "Shae, stay out of sight. Noah, call Deputy Warner and tell him I've got some trespassers…"

Shae stayed back and couldn't stop the painful memories from washing over her once again. The stress of the unwanted attention twelve years ago never truly went away. Even to this day she still got inquiries from journalists or authors who were pining for the next bestseller.

She wrapped her arms around her waist, suddenly cold now that she was in the shadow of the house. Only she feared it wasn't from the lack of sun. Jace's touch had unexpectedly given her a sense of security she hadn't experienced in a very long time.

CHAPTER EIGHT

JACE ENDED UP spending the rest of the morning and early afternoon running off unwanted reporters from his property. It was incredible the way they'd just barged onto private land and parked wherever they wanted. They asked a litany of questions about the search being conducted on his property in connection to the investigation. He informed them they weren't welcome, and that they would have to move to the road where his property line ended.

One of the crews had actually started to drive stakes into the ground for a tent by the time Jace had got over to their location and asked them to leave. Others pointed to those who hadn't moved and had the audacity to say they weren't leaving until everyone else had. He'd had to explain to them in minute detail that once the police arrived he would press charges on anyone he told to vacate and hadn't. Thankfully, that got them moving.

Even after the initial mess, two of the crews had launched drones with cameras to fly over the property. The police had told Jace that they couldn't do anything about the drones unless they flew directly over groups of people or below one hundred feet. Apparently, an Ohio Court of Appeals had already determined that a land owner only controlled that much airspace over their own land. Anything above that height was public, and therefore, controlled by the FAA.

By the time Jace had talked to the authorities about enforcing those rules, the drones had already run out of batteries and the crews had put them away. It never escaped his attention for a moment that his residence was no doubt going to be front page in tomorrow's paper. In fact, he suspected that most of the news networks statewide would run a feature on the latest developments in their series covering the local murders and disappearances. The only thing he'd managed to successfully do was keep Shae's presence hidden from prying eyes. Lance had eventually driven her into town without anyone taking notice.

That last option had left her vehicle at Jace's house, but that was better than the reporters getting a hold of her and demanding a statement. It was a given that Shae would ultimately be cornered, especially after one of the reporters supposedly ran all of the plates on the vehicles near the property. No one said those bloodsuckers didn't do their homework. That didn't mean her presence being announced couldn't be on her timetable. The vultures could wait.

"I would suggest grabbing a sleeping bag from Dad's place and staying at your house tonight," Lance advised after he'd taken a drink out of the water bottle he'd swiped from behind the bar. They were all gathered around a table in the corner of Tiny's Cavern, with the exception of Shae. She was upstairs being interviewed by Detective Kendrick. "I've got a twelve-gauge and some shells in the truck. I'll also give you the name and number of the security company Noah and I used to install our systems. Remember, I even had a break-in prior to my system being installed. A photojournalist broke in to get some sexy snaps of my furnace."

"Trust us, you'll need it." Noah tossed a peanut shell back into the bowl with a scowl. "At least your walls didn't have any bodies inside the drywall and your basement didn't contain any evidence left behind. I'm not sure how that helps Kendrick with his case, but it does go a long way toward helping clear this fictitious Kendall connection."

"The Kendall name was never in need of clearing," their dad said with a stern look. "No one with half a brain ever believed any of that horseshit. We've done nothing wrong. That reporter—Charlene Winston—is the one who made it seem as if we had some kind of nefarious connection to the case. But you are right, Noah. This should bring that part of this horrible story to a close."

"Charlene Winston?" The name wasn't familiar. "I don't believe there was a woman by that name with any of the media crews today."

"That's because that bitch knows better than to show her face around here ever again," Brynn called out from behind the bar.

She was discussing something with one of her employees, reminding Jace of how many things had changed since he'd been gone. Tiny Phifer had been the owner and proprietor of the Cavern for as long as Jace could remember. He'd learned that Brynn had bought the bar from him and his wife, Rose. It wasn't much of a surprise considering that the older couple had taken Brynn in after she'd lost both her parents. The place was truly shaping up.

What was astounding was all the upgrades to the place— such as the pool tables finally being refurbished and the added stage for live music. Even a nostalgic Rockola jukebox had been installed recently with the retro bubbling lights. It played thousands of digital recordings that Brynn could update with regular downloads. Tiny had been old school. His old Wurlitzer, which was still in the corner, probably even had the same CDs it came with. His motto had always been *why fix it if it wasn't broken.*

That particular saying made Jace think of Shae's confession

today. She experienced guilt every time she looked at him. How could she not? She connected Emma's death directly to going to see him the night she was abducted. It made him sick to his stomach. She'd driven into the city the night her sister had gone missing to be with him—and not to say goodbye. How could he have so badly misread her presence that night?

She was riddled with remorse, regardless of how unfounded those emotions were in the grand scheme of things. And she continued to carry that blame around with her to this day.

It made him wonder if she could ever look at him again without reliving that tragedy.

"You need to make a call to the Benson twins," Gus advised around the toothpick in between his lips. He drew Jace back to the conversation at hand. It wasn't any better than trying to rectify the past. Unfortunately, the two went hand in hand. "You had your things shipped to their storage facility, right? TMO paid for temporary storage and local delivery, so maybe they can fit in a delivery tomorrow. In the meantime, you can borrow one of those cots in the basement."

"I'm waiting on a call back from Drew."

The oldest of the Benson twins handled the administrative work while his younger brother supervised the truck crew. They'd taken over the family business, and rather successfully from what Jace had seen. Their site on the east side of town was a maze of modern climate-controlled warehouses now. They even had newer model trucks and security.

"Speaking of moving, how is Reese holding up?" Jace figured she would rather be with them than at school, but she'd started a new job and didn't want to take advantage of the principal's understanding nature concerning the current situation. There had been a few things she'd wanted to get situated in her classroom before Monday morning rolled around.

"I overheard her talking to Detective Kendrick today about some state inspector?"

"Reese has been playing amateur detective." Noah cracked open another peanut, the action itself giving away his opinion on the matter. "I'm not very happy about it. She needs to let the police handle it, especially after what happened with Deputy Wallace out at my place. He was murdered in cold blood, just like those girls. This isn't a game for amateurs."

Gus, Noah, and Lance began talking about the reason why Wallace had been killed, but no one truly had any answers that made sense. They could surmise all they wanted and the end result would remain the same. A deputy had been killed for stumbling onto someone who didn't want to be discovered.

The comment about Reese getting too involved in the investigation hit home, though.

Shae's sister had probably been the first victim, according to what Detective Kendrick believed from the timeline developed by the FBI. Apparently, he'd had some profiler take a look at his case notes. The BAU put together a detailed case file including the information they compiled and correlated from multiple other sources. Jace figured it was only a matter of time before the agency took over. The state had control over the case until such time that they requested the FBI take the lead with its virtually unlimited resources, but would their involvement come soon enough to prevent anymore murders?

Shae's return to Blyth Lake was sure to stir up additional concerns. Jace couldn't help but worry that her quest for answers would lead her down the same path as Emma. From what he'd heard about the residents in town, panic was taking hold and causing the townsfolk to act out in defense of their hearths and homes. Before the fairly recent discovery of Sophia's body, it was rare to see a state police car even pass through Blyth Lake.

Today, Jace had seen three parked outside the sheriff's office.

"How sure is Kendrick that Clayton Schaeffer isn't the guilty party?" Jace asked, wondering why his dad took a sip of the coffee instead of answering the question. As a matter of fact, everyone at the table fell silent. "I mean, he did try to burn Lance's house down. Clay even admitted to having sex with Whitney within the last month. It's not much of a stretch to think he's involved."

"Don't you start," Brynn warned with a pointed finger. She walked up behind Lance and rested her hands on his shoulders. Her blonde eyebrows were practically touching in her disappointment. Did Jace open a can of worms when he wasn't looking? "Everyone in town is pointing fingers at someone. We've known Clay our whole lives. He might not be the most trustworthy guy, but he's not capable of cold-blooded murder. Neither are Miles, Calvin, or Harlan, for that matter."

Jace could see it meant the world to Brynn to believe in her neighbors, but he'd seen firsthand what happened between people who believed blindly in one another. It wasn't pleasant.

"So you think it's someone we don't know?" Jace asked, pausing when Lance shot him a warning glance. He took the subtle caveat in stride. It was in Brynn's nature to protect those she considered family. Jace respected that. "I hope you're right."

Detective Kendrick chose that moment to come downstairs from the studio apartment overhead. He appeared tired, but that was understandable. He'd driven in from the city early this morning and had been going nonstop ever since. It was evident he was committed to solving this case. He wasn't going to lay down and let the FBI take over unless it was absolutely necessary.

"Detective, can I get you a coffee?"

"That would be nice, Ms. Mercer. Thank you." Kendrick

pulled out a chair from underneath the table and joined them, his gaze landing on Jace. "I had an interesting conversation with Ms. Irwin about the party you two attended on the night Emma went missing."

"The party you're referring to was thrown by Nick Caine, a friend of ours who graduated a year before us. I'm not even sure you could call it a party, but more of a get-together that got a little out of hand once the drinking started. I'd had to delay my ship date to boot camp due to getting mono in my senior year. I needed a doctor's release before I could ship." Jace explained again, having already gone over this with Kendrick on the phone. He'd reached out to each of the Kendall siblings after Noah's discovery at the beginning of the summer. "I was flying out that Sunday, and Nick wanted to do something nice for me before I left."

"In the list of names you provided me, you didn't include Kyle Foster."

"Deputy Kyle Foster?" Noah clarified, pushing the bowl of peanuts into the middle of the table. "He's got to be...what? Four or five years older than Mitch? What was Foster doing in the city that night?"

"Kyle Foster wasn't there, as far as I can remember." Jace was confused as to why Shae would say something like that. Had she mistaken someone else for Kyle? "We were at a rental house near the college. One of those row houses. There was only supposed to be ten people in attendance, but you know how that goes when the word got out about a keg. One thing led to another, and maybe we ended up with around twenty or so friends. As Noah mentioned, Kyle was a lot older than the rest of us. I would have noticed had he come anywhere inside the house."

"Shae said she had a brief conversation with him on the

porch." Detective Kendrick leaned back when Brynn returned to the table with a hot cup of coffee. The steam was evident as it evaporated into the air. "Like you, she didn't think anything of it at the time."

"Thought you might want one, too," Brynn murmured in Jace's ear before setting down his very own cup of coffee.

Her kind gesture reminded him of why family and friends were so important.

"What does Kyle Foster being in the city have anything to do with Emma's disappearance, though?" Lance asked, doing so for all of them gathered around. It made no sense from Jace's standpoint as to what connection Foster might have had with Emma. "He wasn't even a deputy back then, and he was also a couple of hours away from Blyth Lake."

"Shae came early." Jace recalled seeing her come through the front door with Stephanie. The two were usually with Andrea, but she'd had other plans that night. He tried to put himself in the detective's frame of mind. "And Foster being there matters because he would have had time to return to Blyth Lake had he known Emma didn't have a car that night."

"You think Foster—"

"There's no way that—"

"I'm not saying Kyle Foster did anything," Detective Kendrick interrupted the various denials going around the table. "I'm putting together a timeline of people's actions and whereabouts, that's all."

"Did Shae say what she and Kyle spoke about that night?"

Detective Kendrick had drunk maybe half his cup of coffee, but he finished the rest of the contents off in one swig. Jace didn't envy the long day ahead of him, but he did want to know if any of this new knowledge put Shae's life in danger.

"I'm sure you'll hear about it soon enough," Detective

Kendrick said wryly, telling Jace that he was now familiar with how small towns worked. He set his empty mug on the table and pushed the chair back as he stood. "Kyle Foster warned Shae that night that she might want to keep a close eye on her little sister. So if you'll excuse me, I'd like to go find out why Foster would issue such advice."

CHAPTER NINE

S HAE DROPPED THE curtain back into place when a knock came at the door. She was expecting Brynn later, who'd offered her a ride back to Jace's house. She'd left her vehicle behind and currently had no other transportation. It didn't matter, though. She was fine with having a front row seat to Main Street where the police station was only a block away from the bar.

Did Kyle Foster have something to do with Emma's disappearance? She didn't believe so. She had dismissed his comment that night as ordinary concern and later as a statement that she thought only stood out because of its context after the abduction. Kyle hadn't meant anything by it.

"Coming," Shae called out, frowning in disappointment that she hadn't seen Detective Kendrick leave the Cavern. What was keeping him from walking over to the police station? "Sorry, I didn't mean to keep…"

Jace Kendall.

Shae couldn't stop the flush that flooded her cheeks. The day's events had wound down with her answering Detective Kendrick's questions, but nothing could wipe away her confession to Jace when they'd been sitting at the edge of his pond. She'd done so in order for him to understand why being in his presence hurt like a physical injury, but now his knowledge was like sprinkling salt over a raw, bleeding wound.

"May I come in?"

Said the spider to the fly. Shae only had herself to blame. She'd put herself in this position. She'd made herself vulnerable by being honest, but she was no longer that teenage girl with a crush. Then again, she'd thought she'd finally worked her way through the guilt of taking the car that fateful night. Maybe she could give him a break.

Memories could be a bitch.

"Let me guess," Shae said wryly, stepping back to give Jace room to cross the threshold. She could play another game of questions and answers. "Detective Kendrick asked if you saw Kyle Foster that night and you're wondering why I didn't say anything earlier. Is that about it?"

"I didn't see him, but that's not why I'm here." Jace waited for Shae to close the door before continuing. Obviously, she wasn't so sure she should have let him in after that response. His warm gaze intimated that there was something more. Her presence here was about closure, nothing else. "I'm worried about you, Shae. From my understanding, there have been some people upset by the finger pointing going on around town. Some unfortunate things have happened where certain people could have gotten very badly hurt. I don't want to see you in the crosshairs of that type of idiotic behavior."

"I'm fine, Jace. Really." Shae's reply didn't seem to be good enough. What did he want from her? She gestured toward the couch, making sure she took the chair. "Look, I wasn't the one pointing fingers at anyone. Detective Kendrick started asking me questions about the night Emma went missing, going over and over those hours before she was taken. I'd honestly forgotten my conversation with Kyle, because I was thinking back to the party itself. Remember, I took the car and Stephanie drove separate. I didn't want to enter the party alone, so I waited out on the porch for Steph. Besides, we were in the city. It shouldn't have mattered who was there at that time."

"It matters if Kyle had time to drive back to Blyth Lake…if he's the guilty party."

Shae understood that Jace was afraid Kyle would come after her, but Detective Kendrick would surely forewarn her if he thought that was a possibility. She sat on the edge of the chair so she could easily rest her elbows on her knees. Jace was close enough that he reached for her hand and held it in his, just as he'd done earlier today.

His gesture was innocent, yet his touch took her back to a time when she'd thought of only herself instead of her sister's needs. It was an endless cycle she wasn't sure could be broken.

"It's doubtful that it means anything," Shae replied, slipping her hand from his as she sat back in her chair. She curled her fingers into her palm to keep his warmth without thinking through the reason why. It was better to talk about the investigation. It was why she'd returned to Blyth Lake in the first place. "Kyle *was* at your party, Jace. He warned me that he overheard some girls say that Emma had a crush on Billy Stanton. I'd already known that, so it wasn't a big deal. No one ever asked me who was at Nick's that night until Detective Kendrick called me a couple of months ago. I listed the names of those I'd remembered and never gave it a second thought."

"Until today," Jace corrected, leaning back and pulling his cell phone from the front pocket of his jeans. He began scrolling through his contacts. "I'll try to touch base with Nick. I haven't talked to him in years and don't even know if the number I have is current, but it's worth a shot."

Shae figured Nick was on Detective Kendrick's list of people to talk to today, but she'd like to have the answers sooner, if possible. Jace was making the call, and he was the one who

Kendrick would blame if this was screwed up. Kyle had always been nice to her, and he'd done nothing that night to suggest he was a cold-blooded killer out to murder her sister.

She pushed herself out of the chair while Jace placed the call. Making them two cups of tea would give her something to do and hopefully stem the urge to look out the window. It wasn't as if she expected some type of riot in the street, anyway.

"Nick? This is Jace Kendall. It's good to hear your voice, man."

She listened closely to the one-sided conversation as she used the microwave to heat two cups of water. Brynn didn't own a kettle. At least, she hadn't left it here if she did, so it was the best Shae could do in the interim of her stay.

"Yes, it's hard to believe it's been that long. I appreciate you coming to Mom's service. It meant a lot."

She winced in shame that she hadn't made it back to Blyth Lake for Mary Kendall's funeral. Shae and her parents had sent flowers, all of them knowing it wasn't nearly enough for a family they'd known most of their lives. It didn't matter that the Irwins had been away from town for nine years at that point. They still should have paid their respects in person.

"Um, I actually called for a specific reason. You see…"

Shae slowly unwrapped two tea bags and began soaking them in each cup as she listened to Jace's side of the conversation. She didn't take him for the sweetener type, so she waited until the tea had steeped enough before removing the small bag of pressed leaves. She added a teaspoon of sugar to hers before carrying both cups into the living room.

"Really?" The surprise evident in Jace's tone told Shae he'd uncovered something useful. She set his tea on the coffee table as he continued talking. He'd stood from the couch and was walking slowly back and forth on the area rug while listening carefully to what Nick had to say about Kyle Foster. "No, I didn't. I appreciate this information, though. I'll pass it on to the state police detective in charge, but I can pretty much guarantee he'll want to hear this from you personally."

"Well?" Shae couldn't stand not knowing what was said on the other end of the line. She sat back down on the chair while he picked up his tea. "What did Nick say?"

"There's a valid reason Kyle was at Nick's house that night. Foster was the one who supplied Nick with the keg," Jace shared, giving the tea an odd look. Did he take his tea with milk? He continued before she could throw out the question. "Remember how most of us used Byron Warner to buy us alcohol back in the day? Well, apparently he said he couldn't drive into the city that night, so Nick paid Kyle fifty bucks to make the delivery himself."

Jace took a drink of his tea and promptly spit the hot liquid back into the cup, but not before he'd inhaled some of the beverage. She sprang from her seat when he began coughing uncontrollably, doing her best to try to take the cup from his hands before he burned himself.

"Are you okay?" Shae realized that was a foolish question as Jace's face became red from lack of oxygen. He was still coughing, but eventually he was able to inhale a bit of air. She took the small gift of his breathing to run over to the counter, thankful that this was a studio apartment. She grabbed a dishtowel and raced back to him so that he could wipe his face and hands. "Jace?"

"Jesus." Jace managed to wheeze out the name, but it sure sounded like criticism to her. He struggled once more to clear his throat before trying to talk. "I think that's the worst coffee I ever drank."

Shae could only stare at him as she allowed his meaning to

finally sink in. Her lone response was to laugh, because his dramatic reaction to her favorite beverage was on par as if she'd fed him a plateful of liver. His face was still beet red from straining to inhale. To make matters worse, he went into another coughing fit trying to clear the liquid from his airway.

She wrapped an arm around her abdomen as her muscles clenched from uncontrollable laughter. It was too much, and the more he looked at her in disbelief, the harder she laughed.

"I could have died," Jace exclaimed, most of his words coming out clear now that he could breathe. Well, she couldn't. Shae wiped away her tears as she tried to relax her stomach muscles, but another incredulous glance from Jace made her attempt futile. "You're mean. Downright mean. What the hell was that crap?"

Shae tried to tell him that she'd made him green tea, but she couldn't get the words out. She needed to sit down before she fell, because at this rate, he'd be taking her to the hospital.

"Stop." Shae held up a hand to prevent him from saying anything else. He was just making her fit of laughter worse by his drawn-out reaction. "Please. I need to breathe."

"You?" Jace asked as he used the towel to swipe away the remaining droplets on his shirt. She thought she heard another wheeze coming from his direction, but she was still attempting to control herself. "I thought the color looked pretty weak. Tea, huh?"

"Green tea," Shae managed to say, using both hands to run her fingers across her cheeks. She might have succeeded in controlling her fits of laughter. "It's one my favorites."

"Of course, it is," Jace said dryly, though his wink told her that he wasn't being mean. She cocked her head to the side in curiosity as she finally sank back in her chair. She didn't know when the last time was that she laughed so hard. "That stuff is beyond bad. You always were the odd duck, Shae."

"Odd duck?" Shae didn't have the energy to take offense and his crooked smile told her she didn't have to. "I'm perfectly normal, thank you."

"Did a psychiatrist just use the term *normal?*" Jace lifted the cup from the coffee table she'd taken from his hands, wiping away the excess moisture. She noticed that when he set the cup back down, it was right next to hers. He was definitely a dedicated coffee drinker. "I usually wouldn't consider going to a head shrinker, but I might make an exception with you."

"And have me know all your deep, dark secrets?" Shae teased, remembering back to when the two of them got locked in the chemistry lab by Andrea their senior year of high school. It was the week before he came down with mono. "Which reminds me. Did Mr. Chandler ever figure out that you switched Lynn's class assignment with yours?"

Jace dropped the dishtowel on the coffee table and reclaimed his spot on the couch. He shot her a look of warning about the secret he'd told her in private.

"No, and you've made your point." Jace smiled as the memory must have come back to him as well. He shook his head in bewilderment. "I never did find out who locked us in that lab."

Shae reached forward for her tea, covering up her embarrassment. Andrea had known of Shae's crush on Jace and thought it had been a good idea to lock them inside a classroom together. There was no need to give Jace any more ammunition than he already had.

"Can we rewind to approximately forty seconds ago when you were smiling?"

"What do you mean?" Shae took a sip of her tea, wishing the calming properties would kick in soon. She blamed herself for the turn this lighthearted conversation had taken, and now she needed to find a way out. "I smile all the time. You must not be looking."

"Trust me, I was looking."

CHAPTER TEN

"**D**O YOU EVER wonder about the choices we made as teenagers?"

Jace tilted the bottle of beer until the wheat-flavored beverage hit his lips. The lawn chairs Lance had brought over from their dad's house had seen better days, but they got the job done. The two chairs were now positioned on the porch so that they could see the driveway and the road approaching from either direction.

"You're asking me that?" Lance propped his boots up on the wooden railing and crossed his arms as he got more comfortable. "I think Brynn was always in the back of my mind. She was my better half, and I left her here all alone."

"Brynn chose to stay here in Blyth Lake," Jace corrected his baby brother, recalling quite well the phone conversation the two of them had after that devastating confrontation. "I'm just saying that our lives would have been different had we not left for the service."

"Do you regret it now?" The disbelief of such a notion was evident in Lance's tone. "Is there something I'm missing here?"

"Of course I don't regret serving my country," Jace said in frustration, hating that he had to explain himself. "You don't find that returning home is messing with your head, even though we did the right thing? What would have happened if Brynn had chosen to go with you? Do you think the two of you would have withstood the harsh reality of the endless deployments or the moving to another state every few years? I guess seeing old friends has me wondering about the choices we made when we were younger."

"Is this about Shae?"

Jace snapped his teeth together instead of answering Lance, because the inevitable questions would have followed. He wasn't ready to talk about Shae. She'd all but escorted him to the door when he'd tried to pay her a compliment. He'd tried telling her in a roundabout way that he'd made a mistake most teenage boys make—ignoring what was right in front of him the whole time.

"Forget it, man." Jace shifted in the chair, wondering how Lance could sit the way he was without hurting his neck. It just went to show that the two years between them made a difference. "I spoke with Nick today. He said that Kyle was in the city the night Emma disappeared because he'd been the one to deliver the keg."

"Paid him fifty bucks," Lance added on, obviously having heard about Jace's phone conversation from Brynn. She'd had the worst timing in knocking on Shae's door as he'd waited for her to reply to his declaration. His offer to drive Shae back to his house had been axed before he'd even finished giving the suggestion. "Do you think he could have driven back and taken Emma? I can't see him being a killer."

"Neither can I, but I'm not so sure Brynn's right to keep her head buried in the sand either." Jace held up his hands in defense when Lance shot him a look of warning. "You know as well as I do that it's most likely someone we know. Kendrick mentioned that Whitney Bell had let someone into her house the night she was taken, which leads him to believe that she knew her killer well enough not to worry about having him in her house alone."

"Jeremy still hasn't gone into the Cavern."

That absence wouldn't be unusual for anyone else in town but Jeremy. Well, maybe their Uncle Jimmy. His fondness for alcohol definitely ranked up there with Jeremy's addiction.

"What about Uncle Jimmy?" Jace had to wonder what Jimmy Webb thought of their homecoming gifts. Jimmy was Mary Kendall's brother and the outcast of the family. His stint in jail and some of his earlier choices hadn't endeared the man to Jace's grandfather—who had been the one to cut Jimmy out of his will. "Have you seen him since you've been home?"

"Yeah, and so has Noah. Uncle Jimmy made his usual empty offer to have dinner, but nothing has panned out so far." Lance lifted his cell phone, which he'd had in his lap, and checked the time. It was getting rather late. "Are you sure you don't need me to get the old 870 out of the truck? A number two shot would make a mess out of any unruly reporter."

"Dad gave me one of his old Remington Model 31s. Speaking of which, did you head down to the station to apply for your concealed carry permit? I need to do that. My old one states that I have thirty days to change addresses." Along with a ton of other things. At least he didn't have the problems that Noah and Lance had upon moving into their new homes. "We should do something for Dad, you know. He and Mom could have used that money for a lot of other things. I still can't believe I'm sitting on the front porch of my new home. It's crazy."

"Tell me about it." Lance drained the rest of his beer before dropping his boots to the ground with a thud. "We'll wait for Gwen and Mitch to come home before doing something. And no, I haven't had time to go see Patty about my concealed carry permit."

"Patty is still running things down there?" It wasn't surprising, but the woman had to be close to her seventies and retirement. Thinking about the station made his thoughts turn back to Shae. Hell, all he'd thought about was that woman since he'd returned home. "Are you sure Shae is safe upstairs all alone in that studio apartment above the bar? Maybe you should suggest she stay at the inn around other folks."

"Is there something going on between you two that I don't know about?"

Jace truly wished he had an answer for his brother. He'd always considered Shae a friend, but her confession this morning had thrown a twist into his reality. Well, saying she altered his perception of certain memories might be a better way to describe what was bouncing around in his head. Maybe talking about it with Lance would lessen his confusion.

"Shae told me something today that I didn't understand." Jace took a swig of his beer to give himself fortification. If Lance spread a word of this to anyone, he wouldn't be walking for a week. "She blames herself for taking the car the night Emma disappeared. Technically, she blames me, because I'm the one she went to see."

"Wait," Lance said with a shake of his head. He appeared just as confused as Jace. "Start from the beginning."

"Shae and Emma got into a fight about who was getting the car that fateful night. Their mom made the final decision that Shae could take it into the city, because Emma was staying in town anyway." Jace couldn't sit still for the rest of this conversation, so he stood and leaned his shoulder against one of the white wooden pillars holding up the porch roof. Lance settled back into the chair that might very well collapse at any moment. "Heated words were exchanged, but Shae took the car anyway."

"Because she was coming to see you at your going away party?" Lance ran a hand down his face in amazement. He held his cell phone and empty beer bottle in the other. "Oh, shit. She remembers that night every time she sees your ugly mug."

"See? Now you aren't helping me out here, man." Jace shouldn't have told Lance anything. Where was Mitch when he was needed? Now he was the one brother who had the ability to analyze a situation and give sound advice. "I don't want to be the reason she thinks of as the first element, but I'm not sure I can keep my distance."

"Keep your…" Lance's voice trailed off as he finally began to fit the various pieces in place. "Oh, I hate to tell you this, buddy, but you're fucked like a duck during the first day of hunting season."

Again, Lance's reaction reminded Jace of why he only ever ran his problems by Mitch.

"There are times when I hate you," Jace muttered, draining his beer. "Just do me the favor of making the suggestion to Shae that she should stay at the inn. It's better that she play it safe, what with everything going on in the past few months. How could it hurt?"

"Look," Lance said, clearly trying to make up for his botched reaction. "Think back to those combat deployments where we few came home with less packs than when we went in. It's hard for me to think of some of my old buddies without remembering the bad times when we were in the shit. Those memories are there, but they're buried underneath the others of when we laughed our asses off because we stole another unit's Humvee or when we put laxatives into the First Sergeant's coffee because he pissed us off with useless horseshit assignments when we were back in garrison, cleaning weapons that were just cleaned."

The good memories outweighed the bad. They had to, or else they would have all gone insane. Unfortunately, the recollections Shae and Jace shared were typical of any teenagers trying to do the best he or she could, given the circumstances.

He thought back to this afternoon when she burst into laughter over his potential death by drowning.

The bonus here was that when he thought of her, he would forever remember that moment now. He wasn't sure why it was so important to him for her to associate his face with something other than a family tragedy, but it was.

"Lance, you might not be so bad after all."

"I get such a bad rap," Lance muttered, standing while managing not to break the old chair. He handed off his empty beer bottle to Jace while maintaining a hold on his phone. "Throw that away for me, would you? I should get back to the bar and help Brynn with last call."

Lance reached the bottom step of the porch when headlights cut through the darkness. Who the hell would be visiting at this hour of the night?

"You might want to go and get that shotgun," Lance advised cautiously, slipping his phone into the back pocket of his jeans as he kept an eye on the approaching vehicle. The movement allowed his hand to remain closer to the holstered weapon attached to his belt. "Who the hell is that at this time of night?"

Jace had already set down the two empty bottles on the bannister, monitoring the situation closely. He finally caught a glimpse of the vehicle when the driver turned the wheels to the right ever so gently in order not to block in Lance's truck.

The light bar on top of the brown and white car gave away the visitor's identity—Deputy Kyle Foster.

CHAPTER ELEVEN

S HAE LET HER gaze drift slowly over the patrons of the Cavern from her spot in the corner. She was looking for someone in particular, but so far, he was a no-show.

The day had been eventful, with her visiting Rose Phifer and Harlan Whitmore. Both had been very good friends of her parents, as well as Chester and Stella. Rose was quite the source of information, especially after sharing that Whitney Bell and Clayton Schaeffer had a thing going on back in high school that had apparently carried over through the years. It made Shae question what else had gone on in Blyth Lake that she wasn't aware of.

"Shae, it's good to see you."

She'd been concentrating on the front entrance and hadn't seen Chad Schaeffer making his way over from the other side of the bar. He'd been playing darts with a dark-haired man who reminded her of Jace, but that wasn't surprising seeing as he'd been on her mind the whole day.

"Chad, it's been a long time." Shae scooted out of the booth she'd claimed around thirty minutes ago and gave him a hug. He'd been friends with Emma and had also been the one to throw the bonfire she'd attended on the night she went missing. "I was sorry to hear about Clayton's recent troubles."

"No one's to blame for Clay's reckless actions but himself, and he knows that." Chad motioned toward the other side of the booth, silently asking if he could join her. She nodded her agreement and wondered if he wouldn't be willing to answer some of her questions. "He could have killed Lance and Brynn, if he'd followed through with that stupidity. You know it's bad when even Wes was trying to get our older brother to see reason. Hell, everyone in town is losing their damned heads over the police asking questions. Someone is bound to get hurt sooner or later."

Shae instinctively wanted to say that people *had* been hurt, but she understood what he meant. Being questioned was enough to cast doubt on one's reputation around here nowadays. The residents of Blyth Lake placed a lot of pride in their surname and the past generations. This wasn't an easy time for any of them.

"How long are you in town for?" Chad asked, leaning his forearms on the table. His dark eyes seemed to measure her response, more so because that wasn't what he really wanted to ask her.

"I don't know." The front door opened, but it was only Harlan and Chester coming in for a drink before their weekly card game. She twirled the straw that was in her glass of water in frustration. She might as well tell Chad what he really wanted to know. "I came back to find answers. Whitney's death means that the same individual who took Emma is still here wandering around free. We obviously missed something back then, and it's time we set it right. Emma didn't deserve to be taken away from a promising life. She once had everything going for her, and then…some scumbag took it all away."

"We never got a chance to talk before you and your parents left town." Chad reached across the table and rested his hand over hers. "There isn't a day that goes by that I don't wonder if Emma wouldn't still be with us if I hadn't thrown that damned bonfire party. I'm sorry, Shae. I truly am."

"It's instinctive for us to think we could have stopped something in our past if we'd only chosen another path or done something differently. I look at it that Emma had the time of her life that night before her luck turned. She was with her friends, she danced by the fire with a boy she had a crush on, and she left there smiling according to everyone who saw her head off into the woods to walk home." Shae might have stretched the truth, but it was evident Chad needed some type of understanding from her. She still played the *what-if* game, knowing full well it wasn't good for her mental health and that it wouldn't change a damned thing. "Now go and finish your game of darts. Your friend is burning a hole through the back of your head."

"Do you want to join us?" Chad offered, squeezing her hand to let her know how much he appreciated their chat. "You don't have to sit here all by your—"

"Am I interrupting?"

Shae was startled by Jace's presence. She wasn't sure where he'd come from, because she'd had her eye on the front door this entire time.

"No, not at all," Chad said smoothly, sliding his hand away from hers. His unexpected wink told her what he thought about her reaction. "We were just catching up. It's good to see you, Jace. How was the Marines?"

"Hard, Chad. God bless the Corps. It's been a long time." Jace shook the man's hand, though he never took his gaze off Shae. It was in that moment that she could literally hear the match sliding on the score of a matchbook. "I didn't mean to rush you off."

There was an intimate suggestion in Jace's tone that made it sound as if there was something between the two of them. Her heart raced at the insinuation. She had to remind herself that he was twelve years too late.

"Not at all." Chad waved off Jace's not so-sincere apology as he stood from the booth. "I've got a game of darts to get back to, so you two enjoy your evening."

Neither she nor Jace corrected Chad on his assumption that this reunion was anything other than two friends bumping into one another. She hadn't even known Jace would be here tonight.

"I didn't expect to see you tonight." Shae tried to concentrate on the comings and goings of the Cavern, but that was made more difficult when Jace took Chad's place in the booth across from her. His right knee brushed against hers, but shifting her body would let him know she was affected by his touch. "How are things at the house? Were you able to get your furniture delivered?"

"The Benson twins showed up this afternoon with the boxes and furniture that I had put into storage, but it's not nearly enough to make a dent in the house." The small tic on the side of Jace's jawline told her that he hadn't stopped by to make small talk. "Listen, Kyle Foster stopped by my place last night around one o'clock in the morning."

Shae was a bit confused by his admission, because she'd run into Kyle this afternoon on her way back from Chester and Stella's house. They'd had an open conversation about the night Emma disappeared, and not once did he seem upset that she'd brought his name up to Detective Kendrick. By Jace's look of concern, it wasn't good.

"Really?" Shae pushed her glass of water away, intent to hear what Jace had to say in case it differed from her discussion with Kyle. "What did he want?"

"Where did you go after you left Nick's house that night?"

The question stunned Shae, for she'd gone over this numerous times with her parents, the police, and even in therapy over the years. She could have easily made it back to Blyth Lake to pick up Emma from the bonfire. She hadn't made that possibly life-saving decision. Why was Kyle bringing it up with Jace and not her?

"I drove over to the collage to meet up with one of my friends who'd told me she was staying on campus that weekend." Shae had done her best over the past twelve years to put all this behind her, and yet here she was…purposefully bringing these long-lost memories to the surface yet again. "She wasn't there, though. She'd changed her mind at the last minute and drove to her parents' house for the weekend."

Shae didn't like the sense of foreboding coming from Jace's side of the table. She still wasn't sure why Kyle would have driven to Jace's house last night, unless…

"Oh, my God," Shae whispered, leaning forward so that her voice didn't carry. "Are you telling me that Kyle Foster thinks that I—"

"Let's just say that he poured that poison into Detective Kendrick's ear."

Shae was glad she hadn't had any alcohol. She would have thrown the contents up all over this table. To have someone believe she could harm her sister in any way was unimaginable to her.

"Jace, I spoke with Kyle today. He was gracious and understanding about my conversation with the police. Why would he go to you and suggest—"

"Foster might be younger than most of the townsfolk in Blyth Lake, but he's old school. He takes after Sheriff Percy, and you know how his life is turning out. You slung mud Foster's way, and he's slinging it right back at you."

"But why go to you?" Shae resisted the urge to pick up her cell phone and call Detective Kendrick. She needed to set things right, but she wouldn't do so while sitting in a bar. "It doesn't make sense."

"It does when you consider the media has hounded my family since Noah discovered Sophia's body in the wall of his house." Jace put things into perspective for her, giving her hope that her presence in town didn't muddy the waters. Detective Kendrick was a smart man. He would see through Foster's attempt to flip the script. Surely, Kendrick was bright enough to know when he was being conned. "I don't believe Kendrick is keeping Deputy Warner or Deputy Foster in the loop after what happened with Sheriff Percy. Let's face it, the man's negligence got Deputy Wallace murdered. Warner might be a good officer, but Foster clocks in and out without caring one wit about the good folks in this town. He apparently wasn't caught up to speed about the fact Kendrick doesn't believe me or my family are involved in Emma's disappearance or Whitney's murder."

Or any of the other missing girls from the stack of photographs Lance had found in the basement of his home. Shae didn't need to state the obvious, though. She was just grateful that Jace had her back. This incident proved to her she needed to help Detective Kendrick in any way she could and to keep trusted friends closer.

"Lance and I made sure Foster understood we wouldn't allow him to run roughshod over you. We made sure he got the message loud and clear." Jace rubbed his fingers over the side of his face, as if the whiskers he hadn't shaved off today were irritating his skin. He looked good, even after a day of moving boxes and furniture. "Do you want to tell me who you're looking for or do I have to guess?"

Shae hadn't realized she'd made her stakeout quite so obvious. And no, she didn't want Jace to know who she wanted to speak with tonight or else he might take offense.

"I paid a visit to Rose and Tiny up at the lake today," Shae shared instead, hoping that she could avoid his question until he joined his brothers who had claimed a table near the bar a couple of minutes ago. "I also spent time with Harlan and his wife. I'm just trying to get caught up with old friends, as well as try to see if they remembered anything from that time. I know Detective Kendrick has spoken to almost everyone in town, but I've come to find out that a familiar face can jog their memories."

"You're doing it again." Jace's searching gaze told her that she hadn't fooled him in the least. It wasn't very nice of him to keep calling her out on it, either. He actually smiled when she pursed her lips in frustration. "Well?"

"I want to talk to Jimmy, if you must know." Jace wanted honesty? Then she'd give him honesty. "Your uncle saw Emma the night she disappeared, coming out of the woods on Seventh Street. Everyone is assuming he was drunk and didn't actually see her. But what if he did? What if everyone is wrong and Jimmy saw something that night that could give us the answers we need to find Emma's body?"

SHAE UNLOCKED THE door to the studio apartment above the bar, thankful that there was a private entrance from downstairs. It beat going outside and around the building in the pouring down rain. She was tired, irritated, and needed a cup of tea that she sure as hell wasn't going to get from a bar.

"Out of town," Shae muttered with disbelief, wondering if that was an excuse Jace gave just so she wouldn't talk to his uncle. Guilt slammed into her at the thought. No, Jace wouldn't lie to her. "Damn it."

Shae tossed her keys and cell phone onto the coffee table as she made her way to the small kitchen. She instinctively walked to the stove, looking for a kettle, only to remember that Brynn didn't leave one in the apartment. Maybe she should make a drive into the city for some essentials. A kettle would sure help her out. It was doubtful that the small grocery store run by Mr. Moore carried kettles or anything but the Celestial Tea brand.

Shae had grown accustomed to British tea over the years, like Leadenhall Street or Bond Street English Breakfast Tea. Each contained a blend of Ceylon and Assam teas that were rich and flavorful.

Thinking of her favorite beverage reminded her of yesterday, when Jace had practically choked to death thinking she'd given him coffee. The memory shouldn't have caused her to smile, but it continued to. He'd asked her out to dinner tomorrow, but she'd politely refused. Their past was their past, and she needed to concentrate on her future.

The cup Shae had used earlier was sitting upside down on a dishtowel. She'd washed it out before leaving this morning, allowing it to air dry. It didn't take her long to fill the cup up with water and set it in the microwave. She pressed the appropriate time that would bring the water to the perfect temperature at which to steep tea—one hundred and seventy-five degrees Fahrenheit. It gave her time to make her way over to the bed to change into something more comfortable. It wasn't like she was going to see anyone else tonight, and the tea needed time to cool naturally to one hundred and sixty.

Shae had managed to unpack a few items from her suitcase this morning. Her sleepwear, which consisted of shorts and t-shirts, were in the small dresser on the far wall. She rested her hand against the top drawer so she could remove her heels when her mind registered the boots lined up against the wall next to her other shoes.

Bile hit the back of her throat.

She struggled to breathe as her eyes locked onto the suede ankle boots she hadn't seen in twelve years.

Emma had borrowed them without asking the night she disappeared.

Someone had gotten inside the apartment. That someone had to be the same person who killed her sister, keeping that pair of boots all this time until they could return them to her.

Shae managed to gain her composure enough to quickly scan the open layout, looking for any hiding spot that would conceal a fully-grown man. She spun around and faced the bathroom, where the door stood half-open. Was he in there, hiding behind the shower curtain?

She didn't stop to think as she ran for the front door.

Shae crossed the threshold and would most likely have stumbled down the steps had Jace not been standing at the top of the staircase to catch her.

She was in his arms before he could ask her what was wrong. Not even the warmth of his embrace could chase away the chill burrowed deep inside at the sight of those boots purposefully placed inside the apartment just as if she'd unpacked them herself.

"Shae?"

Jace would have pushed her away had she not done it herself first. She grabbed his wrist and tried to pull him downstairs. They needed the police. A bubble of hysteria tickled her throat at the thought of calling Kyle Foster, but someone could very well still be inside her bathroom.

"We have to go," Shae said somewhat desperately, quickly moving around him and trying to put distance between them and the possible danger that lurked inside the shadows. "He's inside my apartment. We need to call the—"

"Go downstairs," Jace barked, somehow managing to get his wrist out of her tight grasp. She snatched his shirt, not sure if he understood what she was staying. "Tell Noah and Lance the same—"

"You can't go in there, Jace." Shae desperately tried to tug at his arm once more, needing him to come downstairs with her. This was a matter for the police. "He was inside my apartment. He's probably still in there somewhere."

Shae had been flicking her gaze from him to the open door behind them, checking to see if *he* was coming after them. The nausea that had previously threatened to overtake her was edging ever closer. Why wouldn't Jace listen to her?

"H-he put Emma's boots in there," Shae whispered, her throat closing as another nail was hammered into her belief that Emma was dead. Her mind had always accepted that principle, but her heart would eternally hold out hope. Those boots would forever remain seared into her mind. "He—"

A sob caught in the back of her throat, cutting off her words.

"Stay here."

Jace moved away from her so fast that her fingers never even loosened from her fist before she could stop him. It was then she noticed that he was wearing a holster and the firearm rested in the palm of his hand as he cautiously entered the studio apartment. It had never even occurred to her to grab the one out of her purse.

She held her breath and strained to hear any sounds over the music in the bar below. She was certain that he was in danger.

Twenty seconds later he emerged, his features practically set in stone.

Shae hadn't realized she'd been waiting for him to say she'd imagined it all…that no one had invaded her privacy and a twisted serial killer hadn't left the ankle boots her sister had worn the night she'd disappeared.

She didn't fight him when he took her in his arms, offering her the security she so desperately needed.

Her presence in town had drawn a monster out of hiding.

It took a moment for Shae to recognize the penetrating and raw emotion that washed over her—rage. It was unlike anything she'd ever experienced before, thankfully casting her relentless grief and remorse aside as if they were nothing.

She might have lured a monster from his lair, but he'd awakened something even more terrifying—a woman now bent solely on revenge.

CHAPTER TWELVE

"**I**T DOESN'T LOOK as if the suspect pool has diminished in any way."

Lance was seated a few tables away from where Shae was talking with Detective Kendrick. A forensics team had already come and gone with only one bag of evidence to show for their efforts. The patrons at the bar had been questioned one by one, and now the Cavern sat almost completely empty.

Jace never had any intention of showing Shae the darkness that lived inside his soul. That facet was reserved for enemy combatants. It was put there purposefully through many years of hard training. He needed that part of himself to deal with the environment he'd been forced to live within, and the resulting carnage that combat produced.

The combat veterans that our country developed were never meant to interact with civilians after the crucible. For them to bear witness to the changes the forge had left behind served to set them further apart.

Once the die had been cast, one couldn't unmake the tool he or she was meant to be. Time was powerful process. It was capable of smoothing the harsher edges, however, the metal of men's souls remained.

The uninitiated couldn't possibly begin to understand, because all the living witnesses were cloaked in self-imposed silence. The process we call strife has a beginning and end. The passage of which takes with it the best we had to offer and returned the byproduct of scarred and rendered souls. The only intact souls in this room had gotten up to refresh their beverages, lending a moment's time for the warriors to speak unheard.

"How do you stop yourselves from hunting our adversary?"

It was evident the question had caused his younger brothers to become speechless. That was saying something, but Jace didn't find any humor in what he'd accomplished. He truly wanted an honest answer from them before he decided to take measures into his own hands.

The demented and warped mind of a psychopath had dragged Shae into whatever game he'd been playing the last twelve years…if not longer.

That reality was unacceptable to those who truly knew how to deal with evil.

"It's not our place." Noah leaned forward and tapped the table hard with his finger to make his point. "I don't know what's going on between you and Shae, but this is a matter for the police. Support her, comfort her, protect her…but don't go doing something that will land your ass in jail. This is not a free fire zone. They have rules of engagement here."

"Noah's right." It was clear that Lance wanted to add on an asterisk to that admission. It was rare that Noah and Lance agreed on anything. Instead, he forged ahead to give his brother's advice some credence. "We've all been touched by this, but the smart thing to do is let the police handle the investigation. If this case gets botched because one of us acts outside the law or gets our hands dirty, we would be the ones to blame if the son of a bitch walked free."

"He can't walk if he's in the morgue."

Jace recalled the conversation he'd had with Shae about how she viewed him when they were younger—straight-laced and determined. She was right, in a manner of speaking. Yet she was also very, very wrong.

He didn't play by the rules when the quarry required adaptation to eliminate it.

He'd established his own set of moral imperatives.

"You can tell Brynn that Shae won't be needing the apartment upstairs anymore." Jace stood, not caring when the legs of the chair scraped the hardwood floor. It got the detective's attention. "She'll be staying with me."

Jace pulled out his cell phone and without hesitation, dialed the first number on his list of favorites. He walked across the bar to where the pool tables were located to get some privacy, all the while letting the line ring. There was always one person a sibling could depend on no matter what the stakes—their older brother.

"Jace, how's the homecoming going?" Mitch asked in greeting, his confusion over the call evident. They'd spoken three days ago and would usually go a hell of a lot longer than that between phone conversations. "Uneventful, I hope."

"I wish I could tell you what you wanted to hear, but it's actually just the opposite." Jace and Mitch had numerous discussions in the past over how Noah and Lance always had trouble following them wherever they went. It was true in most cases, but this thing was over the top. What was happening in Blyth Lake was on a much bigger scale than any personal issue they had to deal with in the past. "You've *tapped* out, right? There's nothing holding you there but checking out of the command, right? When does your terminal leave start?"

"What happened?" Mitch didn't bother to answer Jace's questions, but rather he got right to the point. "Are Noah and Lance okay?"

"They're fine, but Shae Irwin returned to town a few days ago. Believe it or not, the same day I arrived back home."

Jace gave Shae a reassuring smile when she looked his way, having done so a few times over the course of her conversation with Detective Kendrick. It wasn't that his comfort was needed. Not in the least. Something had changed in her from the time she'd run into him at the top of the stairs to when he came back out from having searched her apartment. It was something unpredictable, and it sure as hell put him on edge.

"And?" Mitch asked after Jace had fallen silent. He dragged his attention back to the call he'd initiated. "Was Shae hurt?"

"The bastard broke into the studio apartment where she's staying and left behind the boots Emma Irwin was wearing the night she disappeared. He was inside the Cavern, *amongst us,* and nobody noticed anything out of the ordinary." Jace could literally taste the disgust of such an insane action. "Mitch, we need you here. You understand that Sheriff Percy is on suspension. The town will all but force his resignation, if they're given an alternative. Byron Warner has taken over the responsibilities in the interim, but you and I both know he's not up for dealing with something of this magnitude."

"Why does this sound personal?"

Jace fell silent, unable to answer Mitch's question. In reality, he hadn't spoken to Shae at length in over twelve years.

They were old friends who had reminisced about the past.

Nothing more.

And that was a complete lie.

"It is personal," Jace replied honestly, leaning back against the pool table for support. He'd been moving non-stop since early this morning, as well as rearranging furniture and unpacking boxes. He was physically exhausted, but mentally aggravated. That wasn't a good combination. "I'm asking you to come home. Take over the sheriff's position like dad and the rest of the towns' elders are asking of you, and we'll get rid of this bastard that's terrifying our friends and neighbors."

"The Ohio State Police took over the investigation already," Mitch said, his tone suggesting there wasn't anything he could do if he did decide to return to town sooner rather than later. "I've spoken to Detective Kendrick. He seems like a capable investigator, Jace."

"I'm not saying Kendrick isn't doing his job, but no one knows these people like we do, Mitch." Jace didn't have a single doubt that someone from Blyth Lake was responsible for all this bloodshed. No stranger could have gotten inside this bar without someone noticing him. As for the outside perimeter, the most likely avenues of approach were covered by video surveillance. "You can make a difference here. I intend to help you make that difference."

Mitch was silent on the other end of the line. Jace gave his brother the time needed to make a decision. He understood all too well how hard it was to leave one life behind for another. Mitch had been in the Marines for sixteen years.

He would have completed his twenty, but the Marine Corps was putting him out on an early medical retirement. He was more than capable of keeping up with his civilian counterparts, but the pins in his hip would keep from completing a three-mile run anytime soon. His injury put a hitch in his step, but the sense of duty the Corps had instilled in him hadn't erased, nor could it be removed by a few classes given by the transition team assigned to ease his adjustment to civilian life.

Jace used the minute or two to go over the facts in his mind about the day's events. Shae had unpacked early this morning before leaving the apartment to visit old friends. Those boots could have been placed amongst her own shoes at any point during the elapsed twelve-hour period…maybe even longer. No unusual activity was picked up by the security feeds, so that could only mean that one of the patrons who'd stopped in for a drink throughout the day into the early evening was the guilty party. It would have been nearly impossible to avoid the cameras without drawing attention to himself or herself.

"Give me two weeks."

"I'm afraid we don't have two weeks." Jace wasn't going to sugarcoat the situation. "We need someone on the inside of this, Mitch. Kendrick already tried formally questioning anyone and everyone who had a personal connection to this case, and look what happened. Deputy Wallace was murdered in cold blood, Lance and Brynn were almost reduced to nothing but ashes, and the people we grew up with are turning on one another like rats fighting for the last scrap of meat. You and I both know what Kendrick is going to do with the people on the list he's managed to compile from the security cameras."

Jace allowed his words to sink in, taking note that Detective Kendrick was bringing his conversation with Shae to a close. Time was running out before this entire case turned into a royal goat roping rodeo and the governor decided to request the FBI take lead on the investigation. Once the feds took over, the community they loved would never be the same again. It had nothing to do with Kendrick's abilities as a detective, and everything to do with the inner workings of a small town. One just couldn't question the integrity of the whole community without driving some wedges between folks.

"I'll be there tomorrow. They can give me compassionate leave for a family emergency. My last two weeks will be unpaid."

Jace sighed with relief and wasn't even offended when Mitch disconnected their call. He had shit to do, and little time to do it in. His dance card just got filled.

"Thank you, Detective." Shae and Kendrick were both standing by the time Jace reached their table. She had her arms wrapped around her waist, though her chin was tilted upward in confrontation. "As I said, I'm not leaving Blyth Lake. I appreciate your concern, but this is about my family."

"You can reach Shae at my residence." Jace picked up Shae's cell phone and purse she'd set on the table. "She'll be well protected, and I'll make sure she doesn't go anywhere without armed security."

"You don't get to make that decision, Jace."

"I already did. Sue me."

"Jace is right on this one, Ms. Irwin," Detective Kendrick said, warding off an inevitable argument. "An apartment above a bar isn't exactly the most secure location. You got half the town's population in and out of here on a regular basis. It's how this killer was able to gain access to your belongings without anyone being the wiser. I have enough to substantiate putting a cruiser out front, but I think it's time we face the undisputable facts that have been laid out for us—it's more than likely that you all personally know the individual responsible for your sister's disappearance and the murder of Whitney Bell. An officer stationed outside a popular tavern can't stop something from happening should the threat come from someone you allow into your personal space."

Kendrick reached into the inner pocket of his suit jacket, pulling out his cell phone and glancing at the display. From the way his gaze landed on Jace, he pretty much gathered Mitch was giving the good detective a call about the future plans of Blyth Lake and the local sheriff department's involvement. It would be smart for Jace to let his father know that Mitch was returning sooner rather than later. The mayor would be able to appoint Mitch as the sheriff *pro tempore* until such time as a midterm election could be arranged or the next official election was scheduled. Special elections cost money and most small towns avoided them, if at all possible. The town council would have to be involved to determine which avenue they wanted to pursue.

"You're not my keeper, Jace." Shae took her cell phone and her purse, standing in front of him to finish their conversation in private as Kendrick answered his call. "Is this about me telling you why I showed up at Nick's get-together for you? That was twelve years ago, and it was a crush that has long since faded. You know, worn out its mojo. I'm a grown woman who has managed to get this far in my life without having a man make my decisions for me. I appreciate what you—"

"Faded? Worn out its mojo?" Jace closed the space between them, no longer caring who saw them in a compromising position. If he had his way, she'd be spending the night in his bed. Well, he'd most likely be sleeping on the couch from her most recent reaction, but she would still be under his roof. "Shae, you and I could burn this place down with one kiss. And you have it all wrong. I'm not telling you what to do. I'm stating what *I* am going to do—and that is to escort you from this unsecure common area to an environment I can control for security reasons."

"Did I mention I don't like people who can rationalize any situation in their minds to suit their own needs?" Shae asked, not backing down as she met his gaze with her overly stubborn one. It took every ounce of strength he had not to reach for her in front of their friends and his family. "You're edging very close to that category, Jace."

He leaned in close so that only she could hear his confession. His lips barely touched her flushed cheek.

"Now you're beginning to understand the real me, Doc."

CHAPTER THIRTEEN

"WHAT TIME IS your flight due in?"

Shae had awakened to the sound of a morning dove calling out to his mate right after sunrise. All the windows were closed and locked due to the central air and an overzealous security guard, but the dove's melodic cry was still able to penetrate the single pane of glass.

Unfortunately, Shae had tossed and turned for hours before falling to sleep, although it was a fitful one. It wasn't anything she wasn't used to, but last night's events had left her mentally exhausted. She was sure it must be the same for Jace, because he'd been talking to someone on the phone for the last five minutes—regardless of the fact that it was six o'clock in the morning.

"Dad's holding the meeting with the mayor and the other town council members at lunch today, so it should be official by this afternoon."

Shae figured his conversation had to do with Mitch coming home to take over Sheriff Percy's responsibilities. Detective Kendrick had spoken with the oldest of the Kendall siblings, seemingly surprised by the unexpected phone call. Regardless, he indicated that it would be nice to work with someone who had inside knowledge on the town and most of its residents. She was relatively sure this new development was prompted by a call Jace made in the bar while she was distracted.

"Brynn said she kept a copy of the security video feed, but there wasn't a single stranger in the Cavern yesterday. It's someone we know, Mitch."

And that was what Shae was afraid of most of all—that Emma had been killed by someone she knew and trusted. Someone who had helped out on the search parties, maybe even someone who had been in their home eating dinner with their family.

Shae wasn't ready to finish where she and Jace had left off last night, so she tiptoed across the dining room floor to the wooden staircase. They first argued on whether or not she would even accompany him to his new house, but Detective Kendrick was the one to help her see reason. It was hard to do with Jace acting more like a possessive lover than an old friend.

She never should have told him the reason she'd gone to Nick's in the first place. He had totally lost his mind.

What's done was done, and she couldn't change the past. But she could manage this.

That didn't mean Jace got to change the dynamics of their new relationship. It was why he'd slept on the couch last night, and she'd tossed and turned in his bed for the remainder of the evening.

"Going somewhere, Doc?"

Damn it.

Shae had just taken the first step upstairs when his question stopped her from lifting her bare toes off the hardwood floor. The whole *Doc* thing was getting rather annoying. She resigned herself to having another confrontation before her first sip of tea. With a fortifying breath, she turned around with her hand on the banister to find him standing their holding a cup of pure heaven.

"Is that tea?"

"English breakfast tea, to be exact."

Okay, maybe she could tone down her irritation just a smidgen.

Jace was leaning a shoulder against the doorframe of the kitchen, a little more relaxed than she would have expected given the circumstances. It didn't look like he intended to come to her aid. She found she was analyzing every expression and gesture he made, and it was driving her bonkers.

Shae pressed her lips together, resigned that he was making her take the first step. The only reason she was giving in was because of what he held in his hands—no other reason.

"I didn't want to interrupt your phone conversation."

Shae gave a brief explanation of why she had not entered the kitchen earlier. It was clear he'd known she was downstairs the entire time. She slowly crossed the hardwood floor until she was close enough to take the cup of tea from his hand. She permitted herself to take a sip before saying another word. The sweet warmth practically curled her toes.

"I take it I got the right amount of sugar?"

Shae studied him over the rim of her cup, but she couldn't find any evidence that he was making fun of her.

"Yes, thank you." Shae took another fortifying drink. She had quite a lot on her to-do list today, and she didn't want another confrontation. "I take it that Mitch is coming home today?"

"Yes, he is." Jace crossed his arms as if he had all the time in the world. "I thought we could head over to my dad's house this afternoon. It's kind of a welcoming home tradition that we all get together for things like this."

"I'm actually meeting up with some of Emma's old friends this afternoon, but please give my best to Mitch. I'm sure I'll see him around while I'm in town." Especially if she was staying with Jace, but she didn't add on that sentiment to her statement. It would only cause another argument. She didn't intend to be at his house for very long, anyway. "Thank you for my tea. I'm going to—"

"Faded mojo?"

Arousal shot through her with the same exact combo of words he'd questioned her about last night. It was more than apparent he wasn't willing to delay this battle of wills when it would have been the best thing for both of them. She had no choice but to lay out all her cards.

"Jace, you're acting like we were intimately involved in high school. We were only friends. Nothing more." Shae raised her left hand when he attempted to speak. He wanted to talk about this, so he had to hear what she had to say on the matter. "You never would have known about…well, you wouldn't have known about my change of heart had I not told you the reason I went to Nick's house that night. I was seventeen years old and wasn't thinking about anything else but boys back then. That doesn't negate the fact that I was selfish, which is why I told you. I took the car that night knowing full well that Emma wanted it to go to the bonfire with her friends."

Shae left out that getting something of that magnitude off her chest was something she would have told a patient to do as part of his or her therapy. Confronting one's guilt was important in any patient's recovery. She'd done exactly what she would have recommended as a psychiatrist, yet his body language told her it was backfiring into something ten times more explosive than had she maintained her silence.

All the air in her lungs expelled as he closed the distance between them.

"I know about it now," Jace murmured, somehow taking the cup of tea from her hand without spilling a drop. He held it to the side with his left hand as he used his other to palm her cheek. Could he hear how hard her heartbeat was pounding against her chest? "And it's not something I want to ignore any longer."

The world ceased to exist for one singular moment.

The instant that Jace's warm lips covered hers, all that was faded into nothingness. There was no past or future. There was only the here and now.

He tilted her head in order to taste more of her, but it was his flavor that blossomed on her tongue. He was a mixture of mint and dark Arabian coffee. His tongue brushed over her lower lip, leaving behind a coolness that turned scorching hot with another swipe. She couldn't resist the temptation to play.

Shae took control and stepped forward, wrapping her arms around his neck as she stood on her tiptoes and deepened their kiss. His back hit the wall behind him so that the front of her melded to his chest. She didn't stop to think about how he had the use of two hands, but his left arm was now tightly bound around her waist.

It wasn't nearly enough.

She needed more of his touch, his taste, and his—

"Anyone home?"

Shae was grateful that one of them still had their senses, because Jace managed to stop what they were doing and push her behind him before a stranger peered through the screened door she hadn't noticed before. Jace had previously opened the inside door and was obviously expecting the man.

"Yes, we're home," Jace answered, stepping forward and hitting the black lever with the palm of his hand. Shae turned so that the visitor couldn't see that she was still in somewhat shock. What had she been thinking? "I take from the uniform that you're from the security company. My brothers spoke very highly of your system. I apologize we didn't hear your knock, but we were discussing our afternoon plans."

If that was Jace's way of saying he thought they'd spend the rest of the day in bed, he was sorely mistaken. Their kiss had been a mistake. Maybe she'd always subconsciously desired to know what he tasted like or how warm and soft his lips would be against hers. Well, she'd just experienced it and her mind was blown.

That didn't mean she had lost all rational thought.

She was in Blyth Lake for one reason only—to find answers about her sister's disappearance.

Shae caught sight of her cup of tea on a side table she hadn't even realized was located to the right of the kitchen's entrance. She needed the calming beverage now more than ever, so she made sure to grab it before heading for the stairs.

"If you'll excuse me a moment," Jace said to his new guest before Shae had a chance to disappear. He caught hold of her arm right before her foot hit the second step. "Shae, it's not safe for you to be in town on your own. I'll go with you wherever you want to go, but please come to my dad's house this afternoon. If not for your safety, then do it for my sanity."

Had Jace called her by some foolish nickname or tried to bring their kiss into the conversation, she would have told him exactly what he could do with his sanity. But all he did was stand there using his thumb to casually stroke her forearm while staring at her way too patiently with those blue eyes that had a way of prying into her soul—a part of her she wasn't willing to share with anyone.

"I don't want you to think I'm unappreciative. I'm not," Shae replied, slowly moving her arm from underneath his hand. She wasn't so sure why it was so hard for her to finish what she'd set out to say. "But you and I both know that I was in a bar filled with people I grew up with, and yet someone still managed to leave me the boots my sister had on the night she disappeared."

"Which is why you shouldn't be running around town by yourself."

"That's exactly my point, Jace." Shae glanced over his shoulder as a reminder to him that his presence was required elsewhere. She didn't have time to waste, either. "This psychopath can get to me with or without someone around. Why shouldn't I try and make it easy for him?"

CHAPTER FOURTEEN

J ACE SETTLED BACK in the driver's seat of his Range Rover, enjoying the view as Shae strolled across Main Street with purpose. Well, it was technically a determined march with very wide strides. It was evident that she was irritated, but she was the sole person responsible for that fact. He'd done nothing but waste gas all morning long.

The first of September had arrived, but the summer heat still remained to swelter off the asphalt. He'd had to keep his engine running with the air conditioning on for the most part due to the sun beating down on him through the windshield. He was uncomfortable, and she was frustrated when they could both be at his dad's house enjoying a cold beer and grilled steaks.

"You're being completely ridiculous," Shae exclaimed, having fanatically waved her arm around until he took the hint and casually rolled down his window. He wasn't going to show her that his patience was running thin at all. "I'm trying to have lunch with Julie Brigham. We're in broad daylight here. I'm as safe as I can possibly be, so go to your father's house and welcome Mitch home."

"Not without you."

Jace used his finger to pull back on the small lever to roll up his window. He feigned changing the station, all the while observing her reaction from his peripheral vision. *Yeah*, she wasn't very happy. Well, neither was he.

Shae banged her knuckles on the window twice.

"Yes?" Jace turned the volume down on the radio once more to hear what she had to say. "Have you changed your mind, Doc?"

"You know what your problem is?" Shae asked, not waiting for him to respond. She set her fists on either side of her waist to stress what he apparently had wrong with him. "You're bored and lonely. You don't know how to adjust to civilian life, so you're doing anything and everything to avoid the plans you need to make for the future. I've seen it time and time again, and you somehow think latching onto my problems will fill your time until I leave town. I—"

Jace had heard enough, so he calmly turned the key in the ignition until his engine shut off. He then opened the driver's side door, all the while leaving the window down and all but forcing her to back up on the sidewalk to avoid being hit. He ignored her incensed glare as he looked both ways before crossing the street and entering the diner.

"What are you doing?" Shae tried to get in front of him, but he managed to sidestep her when he spotted Julie sitting in the booth. It appeared they were done with their lunch and enjoying dessert. "Jace, you can't—"

"Hi, Julie." Jace reached over the seat where Shae's purse was located, throwing their old friend a smile. "It's been a long time. I hear congratulations are in order for you and Billy."

"Oh, we're just dating," Julie clarified, appearing a bit uncomfortable. Jace figured she and Shae had yet to cover that topic, but they would have to save it for another time. "Listen, I need to borrow Shae for the rest of the afternoon. You don't mind, do you? She'll give you a call later on this evening to reschedule. After what happened last night, I don't feel comfortable leaving her alone here in town. You know, with a serial killer running around on the loose and all."

"I totally understand." Julie tried to wave him off when he set a twenty dollar bill down on the table. "You don't have to do that. I was going to treat Shae to lunch anyway."

"It's my fault she has to cut this short, so please let me pick up the tab." Jace was surprised to find that Shae was no longer standing next to him. The bell jingled above the door to indicate her exit. Damn it. "Shae!"

Jace had done a sweep of the diner before Shae had ever set foot inside the eatery. There were patrons at tables and booths he'd known his entire life, but he was out of time to say hello to any of them. He mumbled his apologies before following in Shae's footsteps.

"Not one word," Shae angrily said as she spun around with her index finger pointed his way. "Does this kind of behavior usually work for you? Do the women you hang around with find that type of attitude attractive? No, don't answer that. I don't want to know what kind of women you socialize with."

Jace would have answered had she not walked across the street to his Range Rover. She yanked open the passenger side door and settled herself inside, leaving him holding her purse. He'd gotten what he'd wanted, and now he would have to live with the consequences.

"Flowers are usually your best option." Tobias Essinger appeared out of nowhere. He was an older gentleman who Jace recalled had an affinity for westerns. According to the book he was carrying around in his hand, that was still the case. "Judith always forgave me after receiving a bouquet of fresh cut flowers. That might work for you."

"I'll take that under advisement, Tobias."

Jace highly doubted that flowers were going to fix his problem. Shae was independent to the nth degree, which he highly respected. She was doing what she felt was right for her, while he was left behind to deal with his own concerns that the killer might very well take what independence she had away by cold-blooded murder.

There was no doubt she'd struck a nerve about the whole civilian thing. She'd taken a potshot at an obvious weakness. He mulled over her accusation as he walked across the street. It was a low ball, even for her by referring to her experience with returning veterans. Given her profession, she understood it wasn't easy to acclimate to civilian life and had played that knowledge to wound him.

"I would absolutely love to spend the next few weeks moving into my new place given to me by my overly generous parents, take my time renovating the barn before the weather turns, all the while spending time with my family while deciding on what I'd like to do with my future," Jace shared with her after settling in behind the steering wheel. He set her purse down on her side of the floorboard before continuing when she normally would have interrupted. "My brothers are adjusting to being home, just like I will, given time and forbearance of the good people of our hometown. Unfortunately, fate has other plans for me at the moment. My main concern is that you don't end up dead like Whitney Bell and that you don't antagonize a vicious killer, regardless that it might very well be your intention. Which, for the record, is exceedingly foolish even with that revolver in your purse. As for my attraction to you? Well, that's a totally separate issue that I'd like to explore at a later time, if you're still alive. So please, don't confuse the two."

Jace turned over the engine, and it wasn't long before he was driving them toward his dad's homestead. He'd had his say, and exchanging arguments over two separate issues wouldn't make this afternoon any more pleasant.

"I apologize for what I said." Shae's words came out as soft as the breeze coming in through the window. The two things almost blended together. "I know you're worried about me, Jace, but I've waited too long for answers. I'll go with you to your dad's place, but you're taking me back to town afterward. I'll give Detective Kendrick a call to tell him that I'll take him up on his offer to have an officer trail me for the next few days. That will solve both our problems."

Jace figured his best course of action was to remain silent. Her solution wouldn't solve anyone's problems, but she didn't want to hear the truth. She'd all but admitted twice now that she would do whatever was needed to draw out this killer. It was as if she were determined to be the next victim.

Well, he would do whatever was necessary to keep her from fulfilling her death wish.

"Let me guess," Shae remarked wryly to Mitch as he took the seat next to her, "Jace sent you over here to talk some sense into me."

Mitch was the oldest of the Kendall siblings, and his dominant aura said as much. Physically, he resembled all his brothers and sisters. Tall, dark hair, blue eyes, and very attractive features. There was no denying that the Kendalls were blessed with gorgeous physical attributes, but they were also fortunate with the endless compassion they all seemed to possess. And while there was something in all of them that broadcasted they were born to lead, Mitch had that quality in spades.

"I wasn't here when Emma went missing." Mitch crossed an ankle over his knee, indicating he didn't mind how long this conversation took. He certainly got straight to the point, though. "I would never assume to imagine the anger and grief your family went through twelve years ago, but your parents don't deserve to lose another daughter because she was too head-strong to listen to sound advice."

They'd all gotten the pleasantries out of the way hours ago, even eating grilled steaks and potatoes larger than her head—not that she ate after having done so with Julie moments before they'd arrived at Gus' residence. It was a welcoming home unlike any she'd ever witnessed before. She'd once heard Brynn refer to the Kendalls as the Waltons. She hadn't been exaggerating in the least bit.

She'd been out to the Kendall residence once or twice for a birthday party here and there during her teenage years. She recalled that Mary Kendall loved lilacs, honeysuckle, and tea roses. The former two were out of season, but the tea roses were still in full bloom and giving off the most beautiful scented fragrance.

Unfortunately, Mitch took that pleasure away from her by driving his point home in a very emotional manner. No parent deserved to go through the grief her parents had experienced back then, and now she was tempting fate.

"You always were a straight shooter." Shae regretted not getting a ride back into town with Brynn. This wasn't a conver-sation she wanted to have right now. "I would never want my parents to go through that grief again, regardless of what you might think. With that said, I'm not a naïve young girl who isn't prepared to defend herself. I'm a grown woman who is taking precautions while I seek to find the answers I've been searching for over the course of the last decade."

Shae didn't want to have this discussion with Mitch or Jace. She wanted more than anything to put down her glass of sweet iced tea and demand Jace take her back into town so that she could retrieve her car. She had things to do, and the Kendall clan had a private family celebration to enjoy.

Mitch had been in the service for sixteen years, and he was finally returning home after sustaining an injury that forced an early retirement. He deserved this time with his family. He shouldn't be worried about her wellbeing. It made her sad to know his homecoming was overshadowed by an evil that had haunted Blyth Lake for far too long.

"I'm sure you've heard the rumors around town, but the board voted me in today as the pro-tem sheriff of Blyth Lake." Mitch wasn't the easiest man to read, and she wasn't sure that trait was a good thing or a bad thing, given his assignment as the town's newest public servant. His expression remained neutral as he continued talking. "In around an hour, I'm heading into town to meet with Deputy Warner, Deputy Foster, and Deputy Perling. Finding Whitney Bell's killer will be our top priority for those who stay under my command."

Shea could only imagine the changes Mitch would implement to the sheriff's department. Glenn Percy hadn't exactly run the tightest ship. The only reason that office had remained afloat or sustained its credibility was because of Patty. That woman certainly had a handle on those deputies.

"You and I both know that whoever killed Whitney is responsible for Emma's disappearance, as well as all those other girls." Shae hated that she had to keep referring to her sister's tragedy as an abduction. They had all accepted Emma's death a long time ago. "I *can* help you, Mitch."

"By opening yourself up to attack and making yourself a sacrificial lamb?" Mitch had already begun shaking his head well before she ever finished speaking. He didn't seem to care that the killer had reached out to her, basically opening a dialogue of conversation. "Coming back to town to take over the reins as sheriff was never my intention, Shae. But I can't in good conscience allow my hometown of Blyth Lake to turn into ruins because no one wanted a thankless job cleaning up after years of neglect. I can't stop you from talking to old friends and neighbors. That's up to you. But don't you think for a second I won't step in if I believe you're putting your life in danger. I'll put your ass in a cell if you start acting foolish."

Shae didn't miss the shared look between Mitch and Jace. They were doing their best to look out for her, but she wasn't their responsibility—not even the new sheriff's responsibility. In the end, it wouldn't matter what any one of them wanted to see as an outcome. Whoever was murdering those young girls had been in control for over twelve years, and she didn't see that changing anytime soon.

"Mitch, whoever took Emma understood exactly what he was doing by leaving those boots in that apartment over the bar. All of you believe we know the killer, as do I. And I have no doubt that the sick bastard thought I would either crumble in my grief or be scared enough to leave town." Shae was willing to make concessions, as proven by her phone call to Detective Kendrick earlier. But she wasn't leaving town. "I'm a professional. I've treated the criminally disturbed in my practice. I can provide insights into his behavior, as well as expand on the profile that you have undoubtedly received from the FBI's Behavioral Analysis Unit at Quantico. I grew up here and have a unique appreciation of the people living in this town. You'd be an idiot not to use my expertise. And I'm willing to continue to stay at Jace's house, but I won't stop visiting those people on my list who I believe may know something that could help us uncover who the killer is pretending to be in the interim."

Mitch nodded his consent, though she wasn't looking for his approval. Something told her that he would be perfectly okay with her leaving town tonight and returning to Lansing,

Michigan.

"I'm meeting Detective Kendrick later this afternoon to go over all the evidence collected up to this point. You and I both know that he can't afford the manpower to have someone follow you around twenty-four-seven. We can all see the state police cruiser at the end of the driveway, but he'll be gone by tonight. I think staying at Jace's house is for the best until we obtain more information on who left those boots for you at your other accommodations. Besides, I know that you and Jace were friends back in the day. Having that kind of friendship and support is invaluable."

Shae was relieved to know that Jace hadn't said a word about what happened this morning to Mitch. Not that they had a personal relationship other than an old friendship Jace now mistook for something more because she'd told him the truth. One kiss didn't change anything. A glance his way had her rethinking that belief, as she caught him studying her from afar.

After their heated argument from earlier, it was a wonder the electricity traveling between the two of them wasn't visible to everyone.

Jace was standing on the sidewalk in front of the porch saying goodbye to Lance, who was heading into Gus' workshop. Well, technically the workspace was used by both of them now that it was a father and son business. Lance was more interested in the fact that Gus had opened the screen door, leaving her to believe that Jace's interest in her discussion with Mitch was for his own self-interest.

She wasn't ready for a man like him. He was everything an alpha male was supposed to be, according to her training.

What made her think she could have handled him as a teenager?

She liked structure. *Strike that*, because so did Jace. She craved easygoing. *Yes*, that was a better description of what she desired from a man. She didn't need someone who constantly kept her off balance. Case in point—Jace's reaction earlier this afternoon. That was totally unacceptable, despite how it warmed her from the inside out to know he truly cared what happened to her.

"Shae?" Mitch calling her name for probably the umpteenth time just proved that Jace upset her equilibrium. She gave him an apologetic smile as she tried to focus on the conversation at hand. "Who else would you like to speak with while you're in town? I'd really like a look at that list, if at all possible."

"Mitch, could I see you in the kitchen?"

For a brief moment, Shae thought Mitch was going to refuse his father's request.

"Of course," Mitch answered, lowering the black boot on his right foot as he prepared to stand. He was sporting a white dress shirt rolled up at the forearms. His darker shade of jeans fit his personality, but all in all, his attire reminded her that he hadn't been home for more than four hours. He had a long evening ahead of him if he were to take over role as sheriff. "Shae, please supply me with that list so that I can compare them to who was at the Cavern last night."

Shae could have answered him immediately, but Mitch was already following his father inside the house. Everyone on her list had been inside the bar at one time or another last night. It was still hard to fathom that someone they all had trusted had absolutely no hold on their sanity.

Motion from where Jace and Lance were standing told her that she was about to have company. Lance seemed to have changed his mind about work and joined Noah and Reese on the other side of the porch, who'd given Mitch time alone with Shae. She wasn't surprised to find Jace joining her, but she was stunned by his admission.

"I'm sorry I caused a scene at the diner. It wasn't fair to you, and I made both of us look ridiculous." Jace leaned forward to rest both of his forearms on his knees. She wanted to tell him to stop, that she didn't need an apology. They were both at fault, because they were both very headstrong. "What I'm not sorry about is worrying about your safety."

"Jace, I'll stay at your place until I decide to return back to Lansing." Shae needed him to understand something first, because she wasn't emotionally capable of handling anything more than what was already on her plate. "As friends, though. Nothing more."

CHAPTER FIFTEEN

J ACE TOOK HIS time walking around the house, noting all the video cameras added to the outside in the form of overhead lights. They had used the existing wiring to power them while replacing the fixtures. No one was gaining access to his property without every second of his or her presence being recorded offsite. Unfortunately, it still didn't provide the security he needed to keep Shae safe while staying under his roof. Security was a matter of layers and denying the perpetrator the opportunities he needed to access the target.

Jace should be grateful to Mitch for talking Shae into residing at his house for the duration of her stay, but he didn't like the barrier she'd put up between them. Of course, the roads they had traveled on over the years had taken different routes. That didn't mean their friendship had faded or that they should ignore the simmering attraction that indicated something more.

"That was a very nice homecoming you and your family gave Mitch today." Shae was sitting out in the open on the top step of his porch, as if she'd been waiting for him to finish his walk around the perimeter. She wasn't doing so just to piss him off. It was clear she wasn't finished going over the rules she'd established in her head. "I'm sorry that I had to be dragged along to something that was meant for family members."

Jace didn't bother to point out that there were other non-family members in attendance to greet Mitch at the house. Brynn was like family and Reese had joined the ranks when she decided to take on Noah as her lesser half, but they still didn't carry the Kendall surname.

"Everyone there was family in every way that counts." Jace wasn't going to sit there and listen to her pick apart relationships and the differences between them. He maintained his distance by standing a few feet in front of the porch steps. "Have you spoken to your parents? Do they understand what happened yesterday? Or are you keeping them in the dark?"

Jace hadn't seen Shae use her cell phone last night or today. He understood about protecting family, but the reverse was also true. It was inherent that a mother and father shield their children from the atrocities of this world.

"I didn't want them to worry, so I've kept it to myself for now." Shae held up her hand when he would have given his opinion on her poor choice. "I'll call them in the morning when enough time has passed to reassure them that nothing else has happened. Them thinking I'm in danger would only either have them asking me to return to Lansing or them making the trip down here. They don't need to be in Blyth Lake right now. They *shouldn't* have to visit the same place their youngest daughter died."

Jace wouldn't argue with her on that point. Neither would he disagree with her assumption Emma had been killed in this town. The boots left for Shae to discover was all the evidence he needed to confirm that Emma was no longer with them and that her killer remained free to slaughter another.

"Mitch called an hour ago." Jace didn't want to talk about the Emma, Sophia, Whitney, or even the case in general. Obsessing over *what ifs* or *what could be*s could very well make a rational person doubt his or her sanity. "Dad gave him the keys to the Decker residence."

"The large plot of land right before the welcome sign?" Shae smiled, telling Jace he did the right thing in talking about something completely different then her reason for being in town. "I always thought that land was magical with its wraparound porch and the white picket fence that goes on for miles."

"You should have heard him, Doc." The nickname he'd used for her slipped right off his tongue, but he wasn't sorry in the least. It suited her. Just as the property chosen for Mitch matched his personality. "I've never heard so much emotion in my brother's voice."

That wasn't technically true. Mitch had spoken at their mother's funeral, and there hadn't been a dry eye left in the church. Jace didn't doubt that was one of the most difficult speeches Mitch had ever given in his life.

Shae's right eyebrow slowly rose and he could see the recognition dawning in her dark gaze under the artificial porch light. He shook his head before she could verbalize what he'd been thinking ever since the phone call.

Though the Decker property was located at the entrance featuring Blyth Lake's welcome sign, the land was still considered part of the town. It was the perfect residence for a newly chosen sheriff, allowing him to watch the comings and goings of those entering his domain. The impeccable selection all but screamed it was cherry-picked with that in mind.

But Mary and Gus Kendall would never presume to interfere with their children's lives. *Right?* Besides Gwen, who had intentionally set the course of her career in finance, Lance was not the only one who had a notion on what to do with his life. His baby brother had constantly followed their father around to *help* in the shop.

Mitch, Noah, and Jace had spoken often about taking a few months after their discharges to figure out what the future held for them and how their lives would unfold. So, if they hadn't known for sure what they would do with their lives after the service, neither had their parents.

Shae's glance to the left made Jace rethink his original assumption. The first time he set eyes on the barn and the large corral made of heavy oak posts culled from the surrounding trees, images of him working with horses immediately sprang to mind. Those large, loving animals gave him a sense of peace he hadn't experienced for many, many years. This plot of land was perfect for raising horses and had supported that type of a business in the past.

Had Mary and Gus truly known their children that well?

"My respect for your parents has hit another plateau," Shae murmured, nodding her head as if she'd just closed a file on a patient. Give her a pair of black-rimmed glasses and a couch, and she'd be right in her element. "You're very lucky, Jace."

He didn't argue that sentiment.

"Let's go inside." Jace had put off a lot of work today to ensure Shae was safe and to spend time with his family. Now that the day was finally coming to a close and she was in a relatively safe place given the addition of the new alarm system, they could relax for some small part. "You can help me pick out furniture on the net."

"What?" Shae was on her feet and already walking toward the screened door. Her next reply made him look twice to see if she'd actually pulled out a pair of spectacles. "Oh, no. This is your new home. You need to choose what fits your personality, not have someone else do it for you. How convenient would that be for you?"

"The office is closed, Doc." Jace reached around her and opened the door, unable to stop a smirk when she shifted so that his arm didn't brush hers. There was no erasing the kiss they'd shared earlier. "I want help with picking out unique pieces that will do this place justice. Now the barn? I have that all mapped out in my mind."

Jace didn't give her time to argue, but instead led the way to the kitchen. He had a small table with four chairs, but he was lacking a dining room set that would seat his entire family with room to spare. Add on the spare bedrooms, the open spaces that could use a side table or two, and he might very well go bankrupt before ever starting the restoration on the barn.

"Dad and Lance will handcraft the odds and ends to put in all the nooks and crannies." Was that a laugh he heard? "But I'll still need some lamps, pictures, vases, and all the accessories that will bring the décor together."

"Oh, you don't want to buy those things from this place," Shae said with a wince, having seen the site he'd had up on his laptop. She slid into one of the chairs before placing two fingers on the integrated mouse. "This house has a lot of character, so you'll want more of the independent stores that have unique items."

Jace opened the bag Rose Phifer had given Brynn, who in turn had handed it to him at Mitch's homecoming party. Rose had mentioned she was heading into the city, so he'd given her cash to purchase a few items he thought would make Shae's stay with him a little more welcoming.

"What's your color scheme?" Shae was clicking away on his laptop while he made her a cup of hot tea and himself a cup of coffee. "Earth tones? I'm assuming pastels are out of the running."

"Definitely earth tones, but I wouldn't mind a splash of color here and there. Maybe burgundy and golds? I saw a picture on a magazine Reese had with her the other day and—."

The kettle's whistle began to shriek until it became a full-fledged scream. He quickly shut it off while avoiding the steam coming out of the spout.

"Where did you get a tea kettle?" Shae asked, her attention drawn to the stove. Her bright smile was all he needed to know he'd done the right thing. "I don't care what anyone says, but heating up a cup of water in the microwave doesn't compare to doing it the old-fashioned way. Jace, thank you. You didn't have to do that."

Jace hadn't purchased her the kettle for any other reason than he wanted her to be happy, but he wasn't above hoping Shae experienced a bit of guilt by putting constraints on their relationship after their heated kiss this morning.

It was simple.

He wanted more, and it had nothing to do with her admission about coming to see him at Nick's party. It had everything to do with the here and now.

"There are a lot of basic things I need to purchase for the house." Jace shrugged off her comment, pouring the hot water over the tea bag he'd set into a cup. He didn't want to get off track and back onto a topic he truly wanted to forget tonight. "Do you see any lamps for the living room? The one I have in there now is ancient."

The evening wore on as Shae miraculously located site after site of possible purchases, from lamps, throw blankets, small rugs, and even wall decorations that didn't include the usual picture frames. Conversation eventually morphed into the design of her apartment, her office, and then eventually more personal components.

"Why haven't you ever married?" Jace set his glass of water on the side table, taking a seat in his favorite overstuffed chair. They'd moved into the living room, ignoring the fact that it was going on midnight. He'd switched over from coffee, knowing full well he wouldn't get much sleep otherwise. "I'd heard you were working at one of the major hospitals in Lansing. I'm surprised that another doctor hasn't put a ring on your finger."

"That would require my consent in most states, and that isn't happening," Shae said rather wryly, her tone indicating that she'd never date a doctor. He had to wonder why, considering she was in the same profession. "The doctors at public and private hospitals work crazy hours and are always on call. It's not conducive to any kind of relationship, nor is it for most of the marriages I've seen disintegrate. Besides, their divorce rate is beyond the stratosphere."

"Sounds like the military." Jace had seen and heard enough horror stories to have shied away from a serious commitment himself. "Though there are some friends of mine who've made their marriages work under extreme circumstances, and then some. These couples are committed, strong, and their support for one another is unwavering."

"I would have to say the same in the marriages I've seen of my colleagues that have made it work. It's not easy. A lot of my patients come to me for that very reason."

"You mean couples therapy?" Jace could see Shae helping couples salvage their marriage. She had great role models in her parents. Those two had made their marriage work in the worst of times, relying on each other through the thick of it. "I'm surprised you work at the hospital. Don't you want your own practice at some point?"

"I do, but the experience I've attained is priceless." Shae had polished off two cups of tea and had declined anything to drink when they'd left the kitchen. She had curled up in the middle of the couch, appearing very comfortable with her feet tucked underneath her. "It's hard to let go of something so good. I work with great coworkers, have regular office hours, and share on-call duties every third weekend. Plus, I'm able to spend time with my parents and have dinner with them every other Sunday."

"Dad started up Sunday dinner here with those of us who are back in town," Jace shared, honestly looking forward to spending quality hours with his family. "It's been a long time since we've gotten to do that. Oh, and Noah has claimed Thursday night for future football gatherings."

"Let me guess," Shae said with a laugh. "Lance chose a Tuesday or a Wednesday for poker night."

"Wednesday is what is being bantered around, but we're all just waiting on Gwen to get back to town. Can you imagine the hell she'd put us through if we started a tradition like that without her here to put in her ante?" Jace was the first to admit that Gwen was the one they all needed to watch out for when it came to the stakes of the game. She had one of the best damned poker faces in the family. "I sure as hell don't want to be on the receiving end of her wrath."

"When does she get into town? I thought I heard your dad mention sometime later this month."

"Last time I spoke with her was the day I drove into town." Jace had disconnected his call with Gwen when he'd driven into the parking lot of the cemetery. It had been her suggestion when he'd commented he wasn't ready to pull up to the homestead without their mother on the porch to greet him. "She mentioned the third week of September, so another three weeks maybe."

"Is she the only one who doesn't know about your mother's final wish to give each of you a home?"

Jace shifted in the chair, not eager to be around when Gwen discovered they'd all kept it a secret—no matter that it was a very special gift. She'd always been the one to seek out the various hiding places their parents would stash their Christmas presents. She loathed surprises, and though she would feel left out because she was the last to know, she would have to accept the reason why.

"I'll take that as a yes," Shae chuckled, setting her elbow on the back of the couch and resting her cheek against her forearm. Jace had honestly never seen her so comfortable and relaxed. "So, we touched on it before, but what are your grand plans for the barn?"

Jace studied her before answering, gauging if her interest was personal or the ingrained part of her professional experience she could never leave behind. After all, once a Marine, always a Marine. He assumed it was the same with any truly professional career. One didn't leave that part of themselves behind.

"You're not talking about my renovations, are you? I wish I had an answer for you and myself, but I have no idea." Jace stretched out his legs and crossed his ankles, enjoying their conversation. It was nice to get to know *her*, versus who she always came across as to everyone else—Emma's sister. "I thought about a horse farm where I can raise a line of quality American quarter horses, lessons for beginner to intermediate riders, and maybe even a place for folks in town to board their animals. Let's face it, there are a ton of people in town who used to ride out at the Happel Horse Farm when they had the place up and running. Now, unless they want to drive thirty miles, they have no place to go. If Rose ever decides to run the summer camp again, I could even provide the riding stock for the summer."

"Then why not give the townsfolk back that special place that you remember as a child?" Shae didn't appear to be asking for any other reason than pure interest. "What's holding you back?"

"Because doing something that I loved as a hobby doesn't

feel much like a job." Jace wasn't so sure he could settle into something he viewed as an enjoyable pastime. "I'm too young to retire, and I don't have the money to stop working."

"Your version of retirement might be skewed by your previous career." Shae settled deeper into the cushions while her lashes fluttered against her cheeks. She was tired, yet he had a feeling she would be wide awake if he suggested she turn in upstairs. Insomnia could be a bitch. "Tell me how the horse ranch would work if you opened it up to the public."

Jace spent the next forty minutes going into detail about the different avenues he could take with a horse ranch. He'd known Shae would eventually drift off into a light slumber. He eventually stopped talking so that he could sit in the peaceful quiet of his living room and watch her sleep.

How many times had he thought about a moment like this when he'd been in the heat of the Afghan sandbox or in the bitter cold heights of the Hindu Kush? He'd pictured a thousand scenarios where he was back home, surrounded by family with a home to call his own.

So how was it that a woman he'd known all his life had somehow materialized as part of his future? Shae had her family and career in Michigan. She'd said numerous times that she wanted nothing to do with Blyth Lake, other than to ultimately find out what happened to her sister.

Why, then, did every unblemished image in his mind going forward include Shae Irwin?

CHAPTER SIXTEEN

SHAE STRETCHED HER arms above her head and inhaled deeply to give herself some motivation to wake up, but the warmth of the blanket was too inviting to throw it aside. She honestly hadn't felt this refreshed in…well, too long to remember. Maybe she should stay snuggled inside this cocoon for a little bit longer.

The abrupt groan that emanated aloud when her elbow connected with a rib told her that she wasn't in bed. Or alone, for that matter.

Shae tried to sit up, but something solid prevented her from achieving success.

"You're one of those, huh?" Jace's voice was raspy with sleep, letting her know the what, where, and who parts of her question. It was the how she'd come to be asleep with him on the couch that had her concerned. "You could have just told me I was snoring. I'm a light sleeper."

"You weren't snoring," Shae said, struggling to sit up. She managed to leverage herself up on an elbow, but it was to find that the living room was still cast in a golden hue from the lamp on the side table. "What time is it? And why are we on the couch sleeping together?"

"We're on the couch because you're not the easiest person to wake up. I had planned to carry you upstairs, but I'm ashamed to say that didn't go the way I'd planned. Hence why I'm on the couch with you." Jace shifted in a way that caused Shae to realize there was no blanket. It had been his heat alone that had given her that sense of security. Her body began to respond to that knowledge in an entirely different manner, and one that she wasn't sure was a wise reaction. "And I figure it's only three in the morning. We haven't been asleep all that long."

Shae briefly wondered why Jace wasn't moving to get away from her now that her upper body wasn't draped on top of him. That was before her brain comprehended that her left leg was snuggled in between his.

"Sorry," Shae muttered, slowly pulling her body away from his in mortification. How embarrassing was it to be caught in such a compromising position? "You should have just woken me. I would have gone upstairs."

"You looked rather peaceful." Jace still didn't move, intensifying the heat that lingered between them. She'd been so immersed with their positions that she hadn't thought to focus on his features. And there was a reason, because his blue gaze captured hers. "How long are we going to fight the inevitable?"

Shae really wished he hadn't asked her such a question, because her body instantly reacted to his intimate suggestion. She was in town for one reason, and one reason alone. It wasn't to satisfy her carnal desire.

The warmth of his hand when his palm cupped her cheek was almost as inviting as the heat from his body, but nothing compared to when he lightly stroked his thumb across her bottom lip. He was opening the floodgate on pent-up emotions, and neither one of them were prepared enough for the repercussions of such a decision.

"I don't belong here," Shae whispered, closing her eyes to prevent herself from seeing his disappointed response. "We both know I'm going back to my life in Lansing when this is all said and done."

"I'm not asking for more than you can give, Shae." Jace brought her forward enough so that he could press a soft kiss against her other cheek. That not-so-innocent act weakened her resolve, because it wasn't nearly enough. She rested her hand on top of his. "If there's anything we've learned over the years, it's that we should live in the here and now."

How long had Shae denied herself that exact philosophy, all due to the guilt that consumed her over the years? She'd never taken the advice she'd given to her patients, even though she'd gone through the detached motions as if she'd healed herself. The penetrating arousal he stirred within her told of just how wrong she was about herself.

She *wanted* to live without remorse.

Shae pushed aside all the doubt and good judgement she used on a daily basis, finally allowing herself to throw caution to the wind. She only allowed herself to feel, and it was the most glorious awareness she'd ever undergone in her thirty-one years.

She took the reins.

Straddling Jace gave her the leverage needed to take what she'd wanted years ago—him. She kissed him as if there was no tomorrow, melding their lips as if they were one. The heat she'd experienced earlier was nothing compared to the inferno that now engulfed her entire being.

Every erogenous zone now ached to be touched, stroked, and caressed by him…only him. Their tongues danced with one another while their hands explored, but it didn't nearly satisfy the ache that had set up residence in her core.

"Doc, we should take this upstairs."

"No," Shae whispered, pulling away long enough to help him sit up in the exact position she needed him to be for what she had in mind. "Do you remember where you were when I arrived at Nick's house?"

"Sitting on the couch with—"

"A girl I'd never seen before." Shae was grateful he'd left the lamp on to provide them some artificial light. She hadn't planned on telling him her fantasy, but this was too perfect. Their situation was too seamless not to take advantage of the moment. "You were sitting just like this, and she was beside you with a drink in her hand. I would have given anything to have traded places with her."

"Why didn't you say something to me?" Jace asked, genuine curiosity lacing his tone. "I would have—"

"Given me one night before you went off to boot camp?" Shae slowly edged his shirt higher over his chest until he helped her free him of the material. She dropped it to the floor with acceptance, her gaze absorbing what she'd only ever imagined. "All I've done is prolong this moment for twelve years, and it will be me who leaves our hometown behind this time."

Shae wasn't sure why she expected Jace to reply, but he remained silent as she slowly ran both her hands up his chest. Whatever the Corps had him doing certainly benefited his health. She traced the contour of his shoulders, his pecs, and eventually his abdomen.

How could he be more impeccable than the man in her dreams?

"Doc?" Her nickname falling off his lips had her meeting his gaze. A small smile met his eyes as he gently took hold of her hands to stop their motion. "The time for words has passed. Let's both take what we can offer each other without regret."

Shae greedily managed another kiss before leaning back far enough to begin undressing, pushing one button after another through their openings. He continued to stare at her fingers with each degree of success. She was finally able to draw either side of her shirt apart, but it was with his help that the soft material brushed over her shoulders.

"Amazingly beautiful," Jace whispered hoarsely, using the pad of his index finger to trace the outer edge of her bra that covered the swell of her breast. Her nipple hardened underneath the fabric, practically begging for his touch. "Tell me what it is you imagined doing on that couch, Doc."

"How about I show you instead," Shae replied, but not before she was able to unfasten the button on his jeans. "Follow my lead, Marine."

Shae deliberately took her time standing before leisurely removing her clothing, relishing the mounting electricity that practically sparked from his darkening blue eyes. Standing in front of him in the nude was absolutely a heady experience. There wasn't a part of her body that his gaze didn't touch in their observation.

She raised an eyebrow in encouragement, waiting for him to remove the rest of his clothing. It was a nice surprise to see him pull a condom from his wallet before letting the leather billfold drop to the floor on top of his jeans. She would have taken the foiled package from his fingers had he not yanked it away at the last minute with a chuckle.

"Not so fast, Doc." Jace wrapped an arm around her waist and spun her around so that it was she sitting on the couch instead of him. This hadn't been part of her fantasy, but she didn't care when he knelt before her. This was so much better. "I have a few delicious fantasies of my own that I'd like to act out."

Shae wasn't about to argue, especially when he lifted her right leg and began to show her exactly what he meant by delicious. She really did try to watch as he made his way from the inside of her ankle to the sensitive area of her thigh, but the stimulating tingles and shivers became too much. He rested her calves on his back as he began to love her in ways that her imagination couldn't possibly begin to visualize.

And when he gradually slid his fingers inside her folds? She didn't even bother to smother the moan that escape her throat nor care that she had a tight hold of his short hair. There was no leverage enough to help her through the escalating arousal.

Jace tongue was circling her clitoris with just enough pressure that the pleasure was immense, but not enough to push her over the edge. She was hanging on by a thread, but nothing she did made him cut her loose.

"Jace…"

"What a perfect angle," Jace whispered in praise, shifting so that her ankles remained leveraged on his shoulders while he positioned himself at her entrance. He'd somehow managed to put on the condom and was ready to take her. This position offered him full access. "Hold on to the cushion behind you, Doc."

Shae gripped the leather, but it didn't give her nearly enough influence over the extreme pleasure that seized her as he began to slowly enter her, not stopping until he was seated within her core…fully. The backs of her legs were resting against his chest as he continued to gradually thrust into her, nowhere near relieving the slight sting of her sheath stretching to accommodate his width. If anything, the light spasms he initiated only became that much stronger.

"It's not enough." Shae cried out when his lips settled around her right nipple, intensifying the mind-blowing awakening of senses. She arched her back the best she could, which only managed to have his shaft slide more effectively over her sweet spot. "Jace!"

Shae couldn't have stopped the tidal wave of her release if

she tried, which had never been her intention. The vulnerable manner in which she was open to him gave her no choice but to embrace the orgasm and ride the endless waves of the beautiful deluge as he began to increase the pace of his rhythm.

By the time he joined her over the precipice, she was floating in an ecstasy that could never have been provided by a simple fantasy. Real life undermined imagination every time.

They had both promised each other there would be no regret, but that didn't mean there wouldn't be repercussions come morning.

CHAPTER SEVENTEEN

"WHAT DO YOU mean, there is an access point from the roof?" Jace asked Mitch, unsuccessfully wiping away the exhaustion from last night. He and Shae had finally managed to move to the bedroom, where they'd made love until the sun began to rise over the horizon. The way the rays colored her porcelain skin to a beautiful golden shade had him rethinking curtains on the upstairs windows. "Don't answer that quite yet. Give me a second."

Jace shoved the filter with the grounds into the slot so that the hot water could brew the sustenance needed to get him through this conversation. He'd already turned on the tea kettle so that the water for Shae's tea would begin to boil.

"Okay," Jace said, able to hold the phone against his ear without fear of dropping it to the floor. He leaned against the counter and pressed his thumb and index finger tightly against his eyes. "Start from the beginning."

"Kendrick and I spent most of last night going over the footage from the bar. No one attempted to take the stairs to the apartment with the exception of Shae, Brynn, and you. That leaves someone breaking in from the outside, but the security camera pointed toward the back of the building picked up nothing." Mitch mentioned at the beginning of the call that he was at the station. The sudden burst of noise over the line indicated that someone had entered his office. "Kendrick and I went over to the Cavern first thing this morning to check for other possible entry points."

"Let me guess," Jace said wryly, pushing off the counter so that he could reach into the cupboard for two cups. "There's a way inside that studio apartment from the roof above."

"In a manner of speaking." Mitch must have put his hand over the desk phone he was using, for the exchange was slightly muffled. Not enough so that Jace didn't recognize Patty's voice. It wasn't long before his brother was back on the line. "Kendrick already had a suspicion that was the point of entry. Forensics processed every access to the upper level, but nothing has come back so far."

Jace recalled there was a small jewelry store of some sort next to the Cavern, but he'd never had reason to go inside before.

"Doesn't Dad do business with that shop making custom jewelry boxes?" Jace pulled out the carafe, having one of those coffee makers that stopped brewing when the pot was taken off the burner. He poured himself a cup before topping it off with an ounce of fresh water to make it drinkable. "Who owns it now?"

"It was passed down to Stella Fields from her grandmother. Kendrick already subpoenaed for the footage from her security system, but it turns out it's useless due to her not wanting to pay the monthly charge for storage of the video data files."

"So how does this help us?"

"It doesn't. But it does open up the suspect pool once more." Mitch made his point, but it couldn't have been the reason he called at zero eight hundred. Jace took a fortifying drink of his coffee so that he could be somewhat prepared for the bomb Mitch was about to drop on what should have been a beautiful morning after. "Would it be possible to have Shae at the station in a couple of hours?"

"What for?" Jace asked cautiously, setting his cup down when the contents failed to do its job. "And spell it out for me, Mitch."

"The profiler who has been helping Kendrick believes she's found a connection between the victims. I need Shae to confirm a few things, and I'd rather it be officially on the record." Mitch was a stickler for the rules, so it wasn't surprising to Jace that his older brother would want all the paperwork in order on a case this size. "Look, this is the last thing I expected to do with my life immediately after getting out CID. I understand why Dad believed he needed to rush me into this, but I truly thought I'd have a few months before making such a monumental decision to take on the responsibility of an entire town. This…this place is a clusterfuck. Patty was able to maintain some semblance of order, but this entire office needs an overhaul in the worst way."

"You can't say that you're not perfect for the role." Jace recalled them as children playing cops and robbers. Mitch was always the sheriff, whereas Lance was the one who always got thrown in jail—which happened to be the treehouse in their backyard. Times were much simpler back then. "Listen, I'll make sure Shae is at the station and—"

"Is everything okay?" Shae asked, though the words were a bit raspy with sleep. She was standing in the middle of the open doorway, using the heel of her hand to rub the sleep out of her eye. She'd somehow acquired one of his t-shirts. It hung well below her waist, but damn if she didn't look sexy as hell. Her gradual smile when she finally focused on him literally took his breath away. "Good morning."

"Morning, Doc," Jace replied softly, eternally grateful for such an ideal greeting. This exchange could have gone a thousand different ways, but this was damn close to perfect. "I made you—"

The high-pitched whistle of the tea kettle finished his sentence.

"I'll get it." Shae shuffled over to the stove in her bare feet, gesturing toward the phone in his hand. Damn it, but he forgot all about Mitch. "You finish up."

"Mitch? Sorry about that." Jace moved a couple steps over so that Shae had room to reach the stove. "Like I said, Shae and I will be at the station in a couple of hours."

"Super Ace, is there something you want to tell me?"

The old nickname practically slammed into Jace's ear.

His first heartbreak had been in the first grade by a pigtailed blonde who had made fun of the poem he'd given her at recess. While Noah and Lance had joked about it on the walk home from school that fateful day, Mitch had played the older brother card just right. He'd laid a hand on Jace's shoulder and explained that love could be cruel and that even Superman had to pretend to be someone else to get the girl.

"Are you saying I should be Superman?"

"No, Jace. Super Ace is what got you into this mess to begin with, because you thought a poem would get Wendy to like you."

"So I should have just given her the candy I got from the basket at Mr. Arlo's store?"

"Exactly."

Jace's current situation wasn't anything like it was now, therefore the nickname didn't apply. He appreciated Mitch's concern, though.

"Nothing to tell," Jace hedged, knowing full well he and Shae had established ground rules last night. This thing between them was temporary. "That doesn't mean I don't appreciate the warning, Mitch. We'll see you in a bit."

Shae faced him while holding her cup of tea with both

hands, already blowing gently on the hot beverage. The sheer bliss that crossed her features on her first sip reminded him of last night. He hardened at the memory, already calculating the time down to the second of when they needed to leave the house.

"Why are we seeing Mitch in a couple of hours?" Shae asked, refreshed by just the taste of her tea. She leaned back against the counter, using her foot to scratch her other knee. The innocent gesture had him wishing he didn't have to answer her question. "Personal or business?"

Jace didn't like the way tension settled in her shoulders as reality began to intrude on their morning. Unfortunately, he couldn't make the start of the day better.

"First," Jace said, not willing to forgo, "a morning kiss."

Jace took his time and savored the sweet flavor of her lips, expressing to her just how much he enjoyed last night.

"Hmmm," Shae replied, resting her forehead against his when they both came up for air. She scrunched her nose in rebuttal. "You're about to ruin my good mood, aren't you?"

"Kendrick is apparently using a profiler on this case, and the woman might have found a connection between the victims." Jace figured he might as well put everything on the table. "Mitch wants us to come into the station to ask you some questions."

Shae surprised him by setting her cup on the counter and wrapping her arms around his waist. He did the same, holding her close and letting her soak up whatever strength she needed to get her through this horrible situation. If he had the ability to take away all her pain, he would have done so in a heartbeat.

"Thank you." Maybe three minutes had passed before she uttered those words. Shae sighed in acceptance, which set him on edge. He prepared himself for the regret she promised they would forgo. "I'm going to take a shower and get dressed."

"Shae, we don't have to—"

"I'd rather get this over with." Shae reached for her cup before she stepped around him to exit the kitchen. "Jace?"

"Yes?"

The hammer was about to be swung.

"Would you like to join me?"

CHAPTER EIGHTEEN

S HAE DIDN'T REGRET a single touch or kiss from last night, and so far, there hadn't been any lasting ramifications. She'd like to keep it that way.

Would he understand?

Honestly, making love with Jace had been the most intimate encounter she'd ever experienced. Her sensitive skin still tingled from the memory, and there was no denying she wanted more time with him.

"You're awfully quiet, Doc." Jace flipped his turn signal up to indicate that he was taking one of the two available visitor parking spots in front of the police station. They could have used the parking lot around back, but neither one of them expected this to take too long. "Something on your mind?"

Shae still wasn't sure how to word her request without him taking offense, but wasn't she always spouting honesty to her patients?

"I don't think we should publicize our…" Shae waved her hand to encompass whatever they'd started between them, not having a name for something so temporary. "I don't want you to take that the wrong way. I just don't want your family getting the wrong idea."

Jace remained silent as he finished parking his Range Rover, even waiting to speak until he'd shifted the gear into park and shut off the engine. Her stomach clenched that he would twist her request into something it wasn't.

"I completely understand. No sense in raising their expectations." Jace palmed his keys, but made no move to open his door. He was watching the front door of the station, his expression causing her to believe he was placating her. "And we can absolutely try it your way. But I'm warning you now, no one knows me better than my family."

Shae would have said that she'd known Emma better than anyone else, too, but she had a sinking feeling that Mitch was about to destroy her illusion. She swallowed the acid back that had taken up residence in her throat ever since they'd gotten inside Jace's vehicle. She'd come home seeking answers, fully believing she was ready to uncover the buried secrets of Emma's past. Now? She wasn't even remotely sure she could handle what was about to be thrown her way.

"As well they should," Shae said, more for her benefit than his. Here she was sermonizing honesty to herself, and she was all but asking him to lie to his family. Returning to Blyth Lake was messing with her mind. She covered her face with her hands to give herself a moment. "I'm sorry. I shouldn't have asked you to—"

"Hey," Jace interrupted, but in a soothing manner that made her wish they'd stayed in bed for the remainder of the day. He wrapped his fingers around her wrist and pulled her arm down to garner her attention. "There is nothing that's going to be said inside that building that you can't handle. Time to saddle up."

Shae inhaled and exhaled deeply, just as she asked her patients to do when confronting something that frightened them. She could do this for her parents. They'd already been through enough, and now it was her turn to shield them from the ugliness.

"No one is saying we have to act one way or another. As for

everyone else, we're old friends. I'm giving you a safe place to stay while you're in town." Jace squeezed her hand in reassurance. "So let's get this over with so you can call and give your mom and dad some answers."

Shae didn't bother to share with him that they weren't expecting answers. They'd long ago resigned themselves to the fact that they would never know what happened the night Emma disappeared. Shae couldn't give up, because doing so would be letting Emma down.

"You didn't tell them about the boots left for you to find, did you?"

"Nope." Shae wasn't in the least apologetic about withholding information from her parents, either. It was in her professional opinion that they'd suffered enough without having to worry about their other daughter. That shot of anger she'd experienced the other night at what this psychopath thought he could get away with returned tenfold. It was time to end his reign of terror, and she'd be glad to offer her help. "I'm ready."

"I never had any doubt," Jace said with a wink, letting go of her hand so that he could exit his vehicle. Shae found herself mesmerized by the sight of the firearm he was carrying, holstered to the belt around his waist. Maybe it was time she got some practice in herself. She picked up her purse and had the strap over her shoulder by the time he'd made it around her side to open her door. The chivalrous gesture brought a smile to her lips. "Don't forget your tea."

Shae reached back into the Range Rover for the to-go cup he'd made her while she'd finished dressing. He was spoiling her, and that technically wasn't a good thing. She was used to fending for herself, and she would eventually have to return to her life in Lansing.

"Let's do this," Shae said, straightening her shoulders and

leading the way to the station's entrance. His hand reached for the handle before she could, opening the door and allowing the smell of stale coffee and leather to wash over her. At least, she hoped the latter scent was leather. "Jace? Who is that?"

A woman with auburn hair was in a heated argument with Detective Kendrick, though Shae couldn't hear their exchange. They were on the far side of the large common area that hadn't been renovated in the twelve years she'd been gone. Four old desks were positioned in twos on either side of the room, with a long table in the back that housed a coffee machine, an outdated fax machine, and what looked to be one of the oldest copiers she'd ever seen. She suspected that it only printed in black and white.

"That's Charlene Winston," Jace muttered, his gaze sweeping the immediate area with disbelief. He eventually focused on the angry woman, who Brynn had described in detail, heading their way. "She's a reporter for one of the local stations. Noah and Lance told me that Brynn all but threw her out of the Cavern one night. Wait. Maybe it was Tiny who had that pleasure. I'm not sure, but I do know she tried connecting the murders to us."

By *us*, Shae assumed he meant the Kendall clan. Charlene Winston didn't even bother to look in their direction as she brushed past them, only to stop short when she realized exactly who had entered the station.

"Shae Irwin?" Charlene pasted a smile on her red lips that resembled the color of blood. "My name is—"

"Not here, Charlene. Please leave." Detective Kendrick had been following close behind, most likely figuring out that the reporter would recognize Emma Irwin's sister. "You'll have to circle around another time."

The reference to a vulture wasn't lost on Charlene, who all but bared her teeth to the detective. Shae could see that the woman loved her job, but there was a sadness in her eyes that was unmistakable.

"I'll do that, Detective." Charlene was well-prepared, reaching into an outside pocket of her purse and pulling out a business card. She flicked it with her manicured nails, holding the small identification just right so that Shae could take possession of it. "I'd love to sit down with you, Ms. Irwin. I believe our conversation could benefit us both."

Charlene left behind a trail of perfume, just enough to take away the pungent odor of stale coffee. Shae was enough of a shoe connoisseur to recognize the brand name. The woman did have good taste in heels.

"Ms. Irwin, I'm sorry about that reporter," Detective Kendrick said on behalf of the department, his eyes lingering on the door longer than necessary. He was holding a mug in his hand that looked older than the detective himself. Shae barely suppressed a shiver of disgust at the stains on the outside of the porcelain. How could he drink out of that pool of bacteria? "The media somehow picked up on what happened to you the other day. I'm fairly certain it will hit the papers tomorrow, but the story will most likely be run on the nightly news tonight."

Shae winced at the knowledge that she would now have to make that dreaded call to her parents. It was one she wanted to avoid, but it appeared Charlene Winston took that choice out of her hands.

"Does she also know why you called me into the station today?" Shae asked, her gaze landing on Mitch. He was standing in the doorway of his office and observing them from afar. She tried not to shift her stance, but something in his expression made her believe he saw what was truly going on between her and his brother.

"No, and I'd like to keep it that way, if you don't mind."

Detective Kendrick motioned that she should walk ahead of him toward Mitch's office. It wasn't like she had a choice. "It's best if we exercise some control over the media, at this point."

"I would agree with that." Jace lifted a hand toward Patty, who was coming out of the small bathroom in the corner. She gave a small cry of joy as she made her way over, even going so far as to cut off Shae's destination. "Patty, it's been a long time. It's good to see you."

"Just look at you," Patty exclaimed, pulling back from the brief hug so that she could rest her hands on either side of his face. "Handsome as ever. Your mama would be so proud of you boys."

Shae forgot that Patty and Mary Kendall had been friends.

"It's your job now to watch out for Mitch," Jace warned with a smile. "You make sure those teenagers raising ruckus up at the lake don't get the best of him."

"Oh, trust me," Patty said with a couple pats to his cheeks. "It isn't the teens that Mitch is going to have to watch out for. It's Rose and what she's going to do to them if she catches them inside those cottages again."

She hadn't wanted Patty's attention to divert away from Jace, but it wasn't like Shae could become invisible. She gave the older woman a smile of recognition. The embrace was unavoidable.

"Shae Irwin, I don't believe my eyes. You've grown into such a beautiful thing, haven't you?" Patty didn't blink twice when Mitch cleared his throat, letting everyone know that the pleasantries were over. "Can I get either one of you a coffee, soda, or water? Mitch has promised me a small kitchen in the near future, but we do have those three beverage choices available."

"I'm relatively sure I didn't use the term *near*." Mitch shook his head, but it was more than apparent he was fond of Patty and vice versa. He ran his fingers through his hair in frustration. "I have a feeling I'll end up doing more renovations to this place than my own home. We should start with a shovel."

"When do I get an invite?" Jace asked, resting his hand on his brother's shoulder good-naturedly. "It was quite a surprise, huh?"

"Mom always did manage to throw a bombshell or two our way. Looks like she got one in on us, now doesn't it?"

"Someone said something to me the other day that has me believing Dad was right there along for the ride," Jace replied, casting a sideways glance toward Shae.

She held up her tea while Jace declined Patty's offer of coffee. Who could blame him after seeing the stained mug Detective Kendrick was using to drink from? It wasn't long before they were all crowded in Mitch's new office. Shae took a seat in one of the two guest chairs, while Jace joined her in the other. Mitch walked around his desk and picked up a pen before allowing Detective Kendrick the floor.

Shae easily read the caution in the detective's stance, almost as if he were preparing for her to react poorly to his upcoming question. She curtailed her need to reach for Jace and seek his support. The heat of Mitch's gaze told her that he was still studying her for some type of reaction, and the last thing she needed was an inquiry about her personal life.

"Ms. Irwin, I've been very upfront with you regarding my presence in Blyth Lake. I was called in to take over Sophia Morton's murder when her body was discovered inside Noah Kendall's house." Detective Kendrick took a drink out of the mug Shae wanted to rip out of his grip. It was easier to focus on that than the fact that he was prolonging the reason of her visit. "I have no doubt that the subsequent disappearance and murder of Whitney Bell is connected to my initial investigation."

"Are you saying that you don't believe Emma's case is related?" Shae asked in disbelief. "The boots my sister borrowed the night she—"

"I'm not saying anything of the kind," Detective Kendrick reassured her, leaning back against a wall that looked no better than the mug he was holding in his hand. Sheriff Percy must have been a prevalent smoker. "Sophia and Whitney both had stated numerous times that they wanted to run away from home. Sophia's father was rather strict and she made it known that she'd rather run away to California to become an actress than stay under his roof. As for Whitney, I'm sure I don't have to tell you about her home life."

Whitney was the daughter of the town drunk. She'd lost her mom when she was young, and Jeremy was left to raise a young girl with an independent streak a mile wide. Jeremy wasn't a bad man, but his lack of guidance had allowed Whitney to spiral out of control. She'd often talked about moving to a big city and becoming famous.

"Emma had no desire to become an actress or to be famous," Shae responded desolately, finally setting her purse on the floor. She held on to her tea as if it could save her from this conversation. "What about the other missing girls? Do you think that man you're looking for is posing as some sort of Hollywood agent or something?"

"No, not at all." Detective Kendrick shared a look with Mitch, indicating that this discussion was about to take a turn. "Ms. Irwin, there's one common denominator between the victims—and that was their desire to run away from home."

CHAPTER NINETEEN

J ACE RESISTED THE urge to rest a hand on Shae's knee to show his support. She'd been very clear that she didn't want their budding relationship broadcasted to anyone outside of themselves, and he understood the reason why. That didn't make it any less easy on him to watch the color drain from her face.

"I take it you've spoken with Brynn or Julie?" Jace didn't wait for Kendrick to answer that question. Instead, he focused on his brother. "Mitch, what about Stanton? He was with Emma that night."

"Detective Kendrick spent the morning speaking with all of Emma's friends, even the ones who moved out of town." Mitch began twirling the pen in his hand, something he used to do when studying for a test. "They couldn't remember a time when Emma said she was unhappy with her home life. We fully believe that Emma was taken by the same man who killed Sophia and Whitney, as well as abducted the other victims, but it would benefit us to know we're on the right track."

"She—" Shae cleared her throat when it was obvious she was still adjusting to this new development. "Emma was very close to our grandmother. She had suffered from multiple mini-strokes and was having a hard time caring for herself. My father wanted her to move into assisted living, but she refused and wanted to stay in her own home. I remember Emma giving my father the silent treatment for a few weeks, but the decision was never made because my grandmother passed away in her sleep shortly after Emma disappeared."

"Ms. Mercer mentioned that as well," Kendrick pondered, but Jace wasn't sure that was the confirmation the detective wanted from this meeting. "Do you recall your sister ever saying she would run away from home if your father followed through with moving his mother into an assisted living home?"

"Emma spent most of that month at my grandmother's house." Shae sat forward on the edge of her chair, curling both hands around the tea Jace had made her that morning. He doubted it was giving her the warmth she was seeking from its contents. "It was the same summer she attended camp, though."

"Which brings us right back to square one," Mitch said with frustration and right as Kendrick received a phone call. "Go ahead and take that. I'll finish up here and then meet you out front. We should take a drive back up to the lake and speak with Rose Phifer."

"I want to speak with Raymond Dixon, too. You got time?" Detective Kendrick didn't wait for Mitch to answer. He already had his phone against his ear, with his coffee in another. "What have you got for me, Kenny?"

Kendrick left the office, leaving Shae to pounce on Mitch regarding the detective's request.

"Raymond?" Shae inquired, her interest snagged by the name of Birdie and Stanley's son. The couple used to own the property around the lake and were the ones who hosted all the summer camps. "I'm supposed to meet with him later today."

"I'm sorry, what did you say?" Jace didn't recall Shae saying she was meeting with anyone today. Hadn't they gone over her safety and that she couldn't just run around town as if she wasn't a target herself? "You didn't mention that on the way into town."

"I didn't want you to rearrange your schedule." Shae shot him a warning look, but she didn't seem to realize that her safety took precedence. "You said that you were meeting with your dad and Lance to go over the pieces of furniture you'd like them to make for the house. Raymond is meeting me at the diner for lunch. You can pick me up on your way back through town."

There wasn't a chance in hell Jace was leaving Shae in town with no transportation. Hell, he wouldn't allow her to be by herself regardless. They'd had this conversation, but she'd apparently forgotten.

"And what if Raymond Dixon is the one who abducted Emma? What if he is the one who killed Sophia and Whitney? Do you think Kendrick's man, who is currently sitting outside in his car and will be doing the same when you're having lunch, is going to have enough split-second reaction time needed should Dixon decide to—"

"What?" Shae asked somewhat abruptly, her attention completely on him. Good. He needed her to see reason. "Abduct me? Kill me in front of everyone while they eat lunch? Splatter blood all over the walls? I'm not irresponsible, Jace. I know how to take precautions."

"Jace, go ahead and drive out to Dad's place." Mitch pointed to the door with his pen. "Kendrick and I will join Shae for her meeting with Dixon. I'll make sure to call you when we're done."

"That's not a good idea," Shae argued with a shake of her head. "We all know how skittish Raymond can be, and he might not talk if he thinks the police believe he might have something to do with all this."

What the hell did Shae think she was doing?

"Mitch, could I have a moment alone with Shae?" Jace didn't even bother to look his brother's way. There was no hiding the fact that things had turned personal between him and Shae, and there were far more pressing issues at hand. "Please?"

Mitch silently rolled back his desk chair, tossing the pen on a mountain of files. He didn't say a word as he quietly walked out of his office.

"We had sex, Jace." Shae stood and set her tea on the corner of the desk, the only clear space on the surface. He didn't miss the trembling in her fingers, but that was most likely due to her rising anger. Well, she could join the club. "We didn't get married, as far as I recall."

"That's not fair," Jace shot back. He had purposefully not brought up last night for this very reason. "What happened between us has nothing to do with me looking out for your safety. I don't give a damn if you need to label my willingness to help you as just an old friendship and pretend we never made love, but you simply can't go around taunting a serial killer into coming after you."

"You know I came back home to find out what happened to Emma. Becoming *briefly* involved with you doesn't change that fact. I'm going to do everything I can to remember details that could help Detective Kendrick, as well as speak with our old friends and neighbors in hopes to jog their memory." Shae took a deep breath, but she wasn't nearly done with her long-winded reply. "Someone knows something, Jace. Maybe your uncle, who saw Emma that night. Maybe Billy Stanton, who danced with my sister at the bonfire. I honestly don't know, but I didn't take a month's leave from the hospital to play tourist in a town I know like the back of my hand."

There were many things Shae mentioned that Jace wanted to address, but her timetable was like a punch to the gut. A month? She'd already used up close to a week. He recalled Brynn saying that Shae was taking an indefinite amount of time from her job, so he never took into consideration that his days with her were quite so restricted.

"I get that you're on a timetable, but I'd like to send you home to your parents in one piece," Jace said softly, not needing to add to his statement. Shae received his message loud and clear from the way she wrapped her arms around her waist. "Doc, is it so hard to believe that I'm looking out for your wellbeing?"

Shae sighed in exhaustion, reminding him that her fatigue wasn't only due to stress. He should have let her get some sleep last night.

"Come here," Jace urged, knowing full well Mitch had closed the door behind him when he vacated the office. Shae stepped into his arms without hesitation. He pressed his lips to her head, wishing he could make her stress disappear. "You'll have answers before you leave town. Kendrick is doing his best, but Mitch knows this town inside and out."

"You act like he hasn't been gone for the last sixteen years," Shae whispered in doubt, her cheek nestled against the fabric of his shirt. "Mitch wasn't even here when Emma went missing, so he's somewhat at a disadvantage."

"And so are you." Jace hated to remind Shae of that small detail, but the past didn't erase the truth. "You entered college that year, Shae. You only visited home on the weekends. Emma was living her own life."

"Someone knows something, Jace."

"Yes, they do." Jace shifted her so that he could gauge her reaction to the follow up of his argument. "And the son of a bitch knows you're here to find answers. He's playing with you, because for some reason he feels safe in doing so. That alone should be all the warning you need to play it safe as well. I'm here for you, Doc. Use me. Let me help."

"You wait until we're in the middle of a police station to say that to me?" Shae said somewhat lightheartedly. He recognized her need to diffuse the tension that had filled the room, but he wasn't going to let her off that easy. "Go visit your dad and Lance. I'll wait for Mitch and Detective Kendrick to join me before walking over to the diner. I have to call my parents anyway, before they hear from someone else that…"

Jace understood that it was hard for Shae to express that her sister's killer had reached out in a sick and twisted way. Explaining the situation to her parents would only have them begging her to return to Michigan. He didn't even question her resolve to see this through, though. She was too stubborn to let anyone run her out of town.

"Excuse me," Mitch interrupted, giving a courtesy knock on his own office door. To his credit, he didn't say a word about Shae being nestled in Jace's arms. "Charlene Winston is doing a live segment outside the station. Now might be a good time to talk to your parents, Shae."

"Shit," Shae muttered, spinning around and reaching inside her purse.

She pulled out her cell phone and initiated the call. Her mother or father must have answered on the first ring, because she pasted a smile to her face and began asking how everything was back in Lansing.

Jace stepped away to give her some privacy, though he second guessed that decision when Mitch quietly followed him out of the office. His older brother always did manage to get the last word in when trying to make his point.

"Super Ace, when are you ever going to learn?"

CHAPTER TWENTY

Three weeks.

THAT'S HOW LONG Shae had been in Blyth Lake, and she was no closer to finding answers than she was the day she arrived home. Whitney Bell's body had still not been found, and there was no new information regarding Emma's disappearance. There had been no more contact by the serial killer. Her life had basically come to a standstill.

"I feel like all I've done is take an extended vacation."

Shae rested the back of her head against Jace's shoulder. She was tired, and the exhaustion wasn't physical. Was this how she was destined to live the rest of her life? Going through the motions in some sort of fog? It scared her to think she had to go back to work soon and leave what little sanity she'd found among the wreckage.

Jace had somehow became her anchor in less time than it had taken him to renovate the lion's share of his new home. He'd included her in decisions she had no business being involved with, both of them knowing those intimate assessments should have been reserved for a long-time lover or even his future wife. Still, she didn't resist the peaceful flow of this short, newfound present that would eventually fade into a familiar stark cold reality.

The beginning of autumn was showing in the foliage and trees. The weather was slowly changing, and the evening hours brought with them an unmistakable chill. It was also a reminder that she couldn't stay here forever. Her life in Michigan was waiting for her impending return.

"Is that such a bad thing?" Jace asked in response to her question, pushing his boot against the porch so that the new bench swung back and forth in a soothing manner. Lance had done an amazing job with the detailed carving on the arms and back of the wood. This home Jace was creating was turning out to be absolutely gorgeous, and it made her sad she wouldn't get to see the finished product. "Taking a break from the carnage you call your life can be a rather healthy endeavor."

Shae playfully rolled her eyes as he tossed her own words back in her face. They'd been talking about his future the other day when she'd said something similar. His dream of what this place could be should absolutely be brought to fruition. He needed to push aside his own doubts to see that creating such a safe haven for others was giving back to the society he fought so hard for in his twelve years in the service.

"I saw that look, Doc. That's not very professional."

Shae laughed before tearing herself away from his body heat and slipping her bare feet inside the flats she'd brought outside with her. The air was rather cool, but she hadn't brought any of her knee-high boots with her. Maybe she'd been subconsciously hoping to find the answers she sought before the weather turned colder. Her smile faded at the thought, but there was no room tonight for anything other than having a bit of fun.

"I can't believe Brynn is actually hosting a karaoke night at the Cavern." Shae couldn't picture Harlan Whitmore or Chester Mayer getting up to sing, but Calvin Arlos and Miles Schaeffer apparently won some type of bet with the duo. She had to wonder if Brynn hadn't had some hand in that pot, because word had it that most of the town was going to stop by for the anticipated show. "How much would it take for you to go up on stage? I might be willing to pay."

His silence had become rather common the last couple of days. It had been hard not to notice that Jace had been a little reserved lately, but it wasn't until he caught her hand and stopped her from walking into the house that he finally fessed up the reason why. It wasn't as if he needed to spell it out for her. She'd known all along what was bothering him, but it wasn't something she could change.

"We should stay home tonight." Jace brought her closer so that she was standing in between his knees. The warmth of his body soaked into hers, reminding her of what they'd created in such a short amount of time. His blue eyes were almost black against the setting sun in his desperate bid to change her mind about going into town this evening. "You and me. We can make some popcorn, put in a movie, and—"

"Hide?" Shae rested her hands on his shoulders, loving the hardness of his muscles and the security he represented. Couldn't he see that their time together was dwindling? She wanted to make the most of the days they had and make memories they could look back on with fondness. "Yes, everyone is going to be at the Cavern tonight. Could one of them be the monster who's torn this town apart? Yes, but you are the last person who I would expect to bury his head in the sand."

"That's where you're wrong. Unlike you, I know how to take precautions." Jace compressed his lips in frustration. "All your presence is going to do is taunt whoever took your sister."

Jace tugged on her arm until she was sitting on his knee. He brushed her hair back and tried his damnedest to convince her that his way was best. It was easy to see he was trying not to incite anger in either one of them, but he was leaving her with little choice but to point out the obvious.

"Those pictures that Lance found in his basement included other girls who have gone missing over the last twelve years. Numerous victims from different towns. What's to say this insane man doesn't follow me back to Michigan? He could be biding his time to come after me when no one is around."

"Are you really going to hand me over a reason to keep you here in Blyth Lake?" Jace shook his head in aggravation, moving so that both of them had to stand. His underlying resentment was finally breaking through. "Mitch should throw your ass into protective custody."

Jace muttered those words as he stood, leaving her no choice but to do the same. He left her waiting on the porch, but she refused to take his bait. She wasn't going to spend time with old friends and neighbors to taunt a killer. She was doing so because she eventually would return to Lansing. It would be nice to say she'd reconnected with deep-rooted friendships.

Besides, nothing had happened during the course of the last couple of weeks to even warrant such a warning. Jace had accompanied her on each visit she paid to those she thought might be able to remember something from so long ago, though her search for answers had netted nothing. No other threats had been given to indicate that her presence had upset the status quo, and they'd had time to enjoy the peaceful evenings at his home.

Shae startled when Jace returned to the porch, having slammed the door a little harder than necessary. He held up his keys, though it wasn't much of a victory.

"I wasn't trying to cause you more worry," Shae explained softly, grabbing his arm when he would have gone down the porch steps. She waited until he faced her, his chiseled features all but telling her nothing she said would change his mind regarding tonight's festivities. "All I'm saying is that if this psychopath wants to get me, he had a hundred ways to do it before now and has multiple ways to go about doing so in the future. Detective Kendrick and Mitch both agree that each of those girls wasn't happy at home, including Whitney Bell. Even though she's a lot older than the other victims, she still resented having to come back home to Blyth Lake and help take care of her father. I'm well-adjusted, and I've never wanted to run away from the love my parents have provided me. He has no reason to come after me."

"The son of a bitch left your dead sister's boots in your room to prove a point, Shae. I heard what Kendrick had to say, too, when we met with him a few days ago. Discovering Sophia's body upset the status quo. This killer is panicking and changing his ways, becoming bolder and taking risks he believes he can get away with in that sick head of his." Jace flipped his keys back so that they didn't interfere when he held her face in the palms of his hands. He then did the very thing she asked her patients to do in every session, only he wasn't her patient. And she wasn't ready for such blatant honesty. "I know that you're leaving in a week or two to go back to Lansing. And I even understand the reason why, but that doesn't mean I don't wish things were different."

"Jace, being here where my sister—"

"Doc, I understand. I truly do." Jace lightly stroked his thumb across her bottom lip, his gaze following the sensual movement. There was a sadness that darkened his blue eyes in a manner that squeezed her heart to the point of pain. "We were both very upfront with where things stood between us, but I find it astounding that you don't even realize you refer to Blyth Lake as home and Lansing only as a place where you reside."

JACE TOOK A drink of the club soda he'd ordered, scanning the bar for anyone looking in Shae's direction. He'd caught a few patrons studying their large table, but that was expected. After all, the Kendalls had caused quite a stir in Blyth Lake recently. Having them all together in one place was just more fodder for tomorrow's gossip wagon.

"What's going on with you two?" Lance asked right before he shoved a nacho filled with cheese and salsa into his mouth. Brynn had added the appetizer to the menu just for him. At least he had the courtesy to wipe his mouth before he followed up with his reason for asking. "Did you not make the bed or something?"

Jace shook his head at how much of an idiot his baby brother could be on any given day. Any other subject would have been fair game, but Shae was off limits.

"Shut up, jarhead." Jace pushed back his chair and headed over to the bar where his father sat with Miles and Calvin. Surprisingly, Jeremy Bell was in his usual spot. "Tell me again why you and Mom didn't stop having kids at Noah?"

"Because then you wouldn't be blessed with a brother like Lance," Gus replied without missing a beat. "And don't think you get a pass on making him that way, either. You kids practically used him as a punching bag."

"We did no such thing." Noah interjected his rebuff as he walked by, having caught only part of the conversation. "Lance wanted to know what punching bags felt like, so who were we to deny his request?"

"Jeremy, I wanted to offer you my condolences," Jace said, holding a hand over the bar for the older man to take. "I'm truly sorry for your loss."

"Thank you, son." Jeremy wrapped his hand around a cup of coffee that definitely looked out of place on the counter. Had the man who'd been the Cavern's most regular customer gone cold turkey and given up drinking? "I suggest you keep a close eye on your old friend. I heard about what happened with the boots. It's only a matter of time before…"

Jeremy let his voice trail off, but his meaning was clear.

"What's wrong?" Gus kept his tone low enough so that the other men couldn't hear over the hum of numerous bar conversations. "Lance can't be the only reason you've come to join us old fogies."

Jace turned so that he could rest an elbow on the high countertop while maintaining a visual on Shae. She was still at the table with Lance, Noah, and Reese. Chad Schaeffer had taken a seat on the far side of the table for the upcoming show of Harlan and Chester singing karaoke, but he was a bit uncomfortable sitting next to Beth Ann and Jack. The newly engaged couple had clearly gotten into a tiff before their arrival.

Well, they could join the club.

"I'm not ready for her to leave, Dad." Jace wasn't sure what made him be so forthcoming with his father in such a crowded place. He really needed someone with a clear head to provide direction, because he was currently lost at sea with a major storm brewing from the west. "It's not like I have anyone else to blame that I allowed myself to get involved with her. I understood the rules."

"Then you know the end of the game." Gus had turned to face Jace, leaving Miles out of the private discussion. "You'll have to accept the outcome, though. Jace, what the Irwins went through was a horrible tragedy that no family should ever have to endure. I can see you care greatly for Shae and vice versa. But put yourself in her shoes for just a moment. Would you want to live in the town that had constant reminders of your sister's disappearance? Of your family's grief?"

Jace wasn't sure what he expected from his father, but it sure as hell was an eye opener. He glanced down at the club soda in his hand, thinking maybe he should have had that initial drink. Alcohol hadn't been on his agenda due to the current circumstances, but he might be changing his mind real soon on that front.

"Lance was always the selfish one," Jace muttered, wondering when he'd turned into his baby brother. "I think I'm digressing."

"Is she who you want to be with, Jace?"

And therein lie the ultimate question.

He hadn't been so connected to another human being in a very long time. He'd been involved a time or two in semi-serious relationships over the course of his life, but those affairs had fizzled out with each deployment. His homecoming and Shae's presence had somehow merged into one event in his head.

He honestly wasn't sure what he would do with himself once she went back to her life in Lansing. Yes, he'd pointed out to her that she referred to Blyth Lake as home, but that little nuance didn't matter a bit if she wasn't happy.

Had they started something that could be lasting if given the time to tend to their feelings for one another? He could admit to wanting to find out, but at what cost? Could they sustain a long-distance relationship? Was he willing to move away from home, after doing everything in his power to make it back here to his family?

Jace didn't bother to answer his dad's question. Instead, he studied Shae as she stood from the table and made her way over to speak to Chester's wife. Stella's hands were telling their own story as she became very animated about the topic of conversation.

The front door opened to reveal a friend of Chad Schaeffer.

"Dad, isn't that the new owner of the garage a block over?" Jace asked, noticing that the man surveyed the room in a manner that was only taught in the service. "Lance mentioned that Mr. Delaney died from a heart attack, but is that guy related to the family?"

"Irish? He's new to town. Quiet type, minds his manners, and doesn't spread shoptalk."

So in other words, the outsider was accepted based on the fact that no one needed to worry about airing their dirty laundry when driving their vehicles in for an oil change. It didn't hurt that Chad Schaeffer appeared to be a close buddy of some sort.

Jace did his best not to show his displeasure when Irish's gaze landed on Shae. The man's interest was brief, but it was there nonetheless.

A loud protest from Shae had Jace slamming his club soda on the hard surface of the bar and taking a step forward before his mind had time to process what was really happening across the room. Stella was trying to coax Shae up to the microphone to kick off karaoke night, but she was very stubborn and set in her ways. It didn't surprise him when Shae pulled Rose out of her seat and pushed the older woman toward the stage.

Shae immediately bowed to the cheering crowd at the feat she'd accomplished, because everyone in town was well aware Rose didn't sing in front of people. Her smile brightened the room and as their stares connected, it was easy to forget their earlier argument.

Jace wanted nothing more than to close the distance between them and let the entire population of Blyth Lake know that she was his...only she wasn't. And the chances were she never would be.

CHAPTER TWENTY-ONE

"**H**EADACHE?"

"Only when you talk," Shae muttered, making her way over to the stove. She'd meant any slightest sound made her head throb to the beat of her heart, but her reply sure as hell came out bitchy. "I didn't mean—"

"I know what you meant, Doc."

Jace's light laughter rang out through the kitchen, but it was a soothing sound more than anything. She hated that they'd spent most of last night on non-speaking terms. They'd let their guards down toward the later part of the evening, but that might have had something to do with the amount of alcohol she'd consumed after some goading by Beth Ann.

The sight of a cup filled with tea awaited her on the counter. Her attempt to smooth things over in the light of day went by the wayside, because it was apparently not needed.

"I'd walk over there to hug you, but my head might explode on impact."

"I wanted to make sure you were okay before I head into the city to look at that lumber." Jace was in the process of grabbing his sunglasses and wallet off the kitchen table, but his blue eyes regarded her skeptically after she'd turned to face him. "You think you're up for making the drive with me?"

Shae closed her eyes as the throbbing in her temples remained steady, though the warmth of the cup in her hands mitigated the waves of nausea in her stomach. She'd be okay in an hour once the pain reliever kicked in, but she definitely wasn't up for that long of a drive.

"I'll take that as a no."

"I'll take a kiss," Shae offered up, hoping he understood exactly what she meant by that invitation. She didn't want to spend the week she had left by arguing with him. It had been very hard for her to accept over the course of her stay that she was no longer going to find the answers she'd thought might finally be within her grasp. She'd found something else entirely, and she wasn't so sure what to do with the diamond she'd found amongst the coal. "I took a shower and brushed my teeth."

"That's my incentive, huh?" Jace didn't hesitate, though. He strolled over and trapped her against the kitchen counter, leaning in so that his lips were inches from hers. How was it that he could still send tingles all the way down to her toes after all this time? He surprised her when he didn't steal the kiss she'd offered. "Doc, I understand."

Shae wasn't in the right frame of mind to have this conversation. Her grip tightened on the mug and her throat constricted due to the overwhelming sorrow that now surrounded them.

He was letting her go.

And he understood her reason why it had to be this way.

Shae blamed her inability to speak due to the fact that she'd had too much to drink the night before. She always became overly emotional after too much alcohol, and this moment was no exception.

Jace took the cup of tea from her hands and set it behind her on the counter. He pulled her into his embrace and held her as a few teardrops escaped, though this time it had nothing to do with the loss of her sister.

"I want you to know something, Shae Irwin." Jace's tone

became thick with the sentiment he was conveying. "I missed out on what you had to offer all those years ago. You are an extraordinary woman filled with strength and grace who will always hold a special place in my heart, and I'll thank God for the rest of my life that we had this time together."

Shae nodded, but she still couldn't speak. Her tears wouldn't stop. What was it about this town and goodbyes?

"I'm not going to ruin what time we have left by pouting like a teenage boy who didn't win the State title." Jace continued to stroke her back with his comforting touch, reminding her that she would no longer have him to lean on when her days didn't go quite as planned. "I'll continue to help you search for answers regarding Emma's disappearance, but we're going to spend the remainder of your time here enjoying every other second of the day and night. Are you with me?"

"I'm with you, Jace," Shae whispered, tilting her head up to receive the kiss she'd asked for earlier.

The small lines at the corners of his eyes crinkled as he smiled, though that didn't stop him from softly pressing his lips to hers. The firm way he took control of the situation sent arousal shooting through her, and she was sitting on the counter before she even realized he'd had his hands underneath her arms.

Jace tore his lips from hers, but only to follow her jawline and the curve of her neck. She dug her fingers into his shoulders as he went a little lower, taking with him her loose t-shirt until he'd bared her shoulder. The light nibble of his teeth had her wondering what it would take to keep him home today.

"I'll make sure to buy another box of condoms while I'm out," Jace muttered, finally giving her reason to allow reality to intrude on this moment. His large hands were now resting on her thighs, which were bare due to the shorts she was wearing.

"I should be back by early afternoon."

Shae's headache came back full force when she realized she'd set up a lunch meeting with Jace's uncle. Those plans had been made when Jimmy Webb had shown up at the Cavern right before Harlan and Chester took the stage. She hadn't shared the news with Jace.

"Okay," Shae whispered, letting her hands slide down the front of him as he stepped back. She offered him a wary smile, thinking it might be a good thing she hadn't told him of her plans. "Drive safe."

"Always do, Doc."

Jace reached for his sunglasses and wallet he'd set on the counter next to her tea, giving her a quick wink. She wiped away what moisture was left on her cheeks and watched the way he sauntered through the doorway. She wanted to have fun with him later, but the guilt of withholding something that could inadvertently affect him would eat her alive if she didn't come clean.

"Jace?" Shae quickly hopped off the counter, wincing when the throbbing in her temples magnified with the movement. "Wait!"

Jace was waiting for her by the front door, his sunglasses already positioned on the bridge of his nose. The darkened lenses hid his blue eyes, but that wasn't a bad thing. She wouldn't be able to see his censure.

"I'm meeting your uncle at the diner for lunch." Shae held her breath and waited for the warnings as to why that was such a bad idea. Detective Kendrick had to pull the officer that had been guarding her sometime last week when no other incidents occurred to back up his claim to his superiors that she was in danger. Jace's counsel never came, so she followed up her admission with why the location would be safe. "I'll be at

Annie's Diner, where I know practically everyone. And besides, he's your uncle."

"I know you'll take every precaution to stay safe." Jace lifted up one side of his mouth in an endearing smile. "See? I'm doing my best to hold up my end of the bargain."

Jace gave her a two-finger salute before he walked out the front door. He was talking about their last week together and how they should relish every second given. And yes, he was also trying to give her some space and a little leeway to do what she'd come home to do. She still walked across the hardwood floor to throw the deadbolt, knowing full well he was waiting at the top of the porch steps to hear the latching of the lock.

Home.

Jace was right.

She did refer to Blyth Lake as home.

She sighed in regret as her hand dropped from the door. It didn't matter how she viewed the town, though. Emma was everywhere. At the diner eating a banana split when their mom took them to celebrate the end of the school year, at the bank when she would ask for a lollipop from the teller, and at the lake where she would fearlessly jump off the pier. Every square inch of Blyth Lake was doused in memories of her sister. The air itself was somewhat overwhelming.

The incessant throbbing of Shae's temples reminded her that she'd left a perfectly good cup of tea on the counter. She made her way back into the kitchen where her liquid sanity had now gone cold. Setting it in the microwave, she thought about the day ahead.

Would Jimmy Webb have answers that had somehow gone overlooked all these years?

It was doubtful, but it was still a checkmark on the list Shae had mentally created on the drive from Michigan to Ohio. She would still be able to say that she'd finally done all she could to find closure as she drove away from home and left everything behind once again.

CHAPTER TWENTY-TWO

JACE INSTINCTIVELY TURNED the radio down when a line of brake lights appeared before him. He grimaced as he slowly pressed on the pedal to slow his Range Rover.

Damn it.

He tapped the display in the middle of the dashboard to bring up his list of contacts via Bluetooth. Choosing Mitch's name amongst his siblings, he waited impatiently for his older brother to pick up the line. There was a benefit to knowing the sheriff in Blyth Lake, and Jace wasn't above using that contact when the need arose.

"What's up, Jace?"

"Are you in town?"

The chances of Mitch being anywhere else, even his new home, were zero to none. The man had always been a workaholic, and this important role he'd undertaken would get all the attention it deserved.

"No," Mitch replied, his irritation evident. "I'm out at Raymond Dixon's ranch, trying to get him to see reason. Is there an emergency?"

"No," Jace answered, thinking better of asking his older brother to have lunch at the diner to watch over Shae. He was being overprotective, just as she'd said multiple times before. She was in a public place, surrounded by old friends and neighbors who would never allow something to happen to her.

They'd all know to keep a close eye on her due to the circumstances. "It's nothing. What's going on over at Raymond's place?"

"The son of a bitch is holed up in his house with his girlfriend, claiming that she told tell the police that he was the one who killed Whitney Bell and those other girls." It was clear that Mitch didn't believe that for a second, but something had to have happened to cause Raymond to do something so crazy. Then again, Raymond always did have a screw loose. "Apparently, they got into a fight over whether or not Worcestershire sauce should be kept in the refrigerator. One thing led to another, and Celeste threatened to tell the police he murdered Whitney."

Jace was glad that traffic had come to a full stop in the left lane or else he probably would have driven into the median. Mitch had to be pulling his leg.

"You're joking, right?"

"I wish," Mitch muttered, a breeze aiding in the distortion of his words. "Celeste freaked out when she realized she'd pushed the crazy bastard a little too far. She called Patty, and now the Dixon ranch is surrounded by my deputies. Raymond is demanding in writing that we believe his innocence before he lets her out of that house. And trust me, Celeste will have a bag in her hand when she does, because I refuse to let her go back to that asshole. I never liked the son of a bitch, anyway."

Jace truly hoped Mitch could get Celeste to see reason. She was older than they were by quite a few years and had always been nice in her own way. It appeared that side of her had been wiped away after all the years spent with someone like Raymond. Granted, the threat she issued was quite disgusting and downright abhorrent. Responsibility for who they turned out to be lay at both their feet.

Bottom line? They weren't good for each other.

"I'll let you go to deal with the crazies." Jace was thankful he had no desire to enter the type of career that put him in the path of uncontrollable events and insane people. "Good luck. It sounds like you're going to need it. Oh, and Worcestershire sauce should be refrigerated. You know, in case you still need to settle that argument."

"No, it doesn't," Mitch replied with irritation that bordered on downright anger. "It says no such thing on the label. I forget that you can be an ass sometimes."

Jace would have argued that Mitch was thinking of their baby brother, but the line went dead.

Priorities.

There was no doubt this argument would come up again at some point, but it certainly wouldn't end in a hostage situation.

Jace gradually lifted his foot off the brake pedal when the bumpers in front of him began to slowly roll forward…no more than twenty feet. *Damn it.* Another glance at the clock on the dashboard told him there was no way in hell he was going to make that lunch meeting.

It wasn't like anything had happened over the course of the last few weeks. In fact, it had been a little too quiet. From his understanding, Deputy Wallace was murdered on Noah's property right after Sophia Morton's body was found inside his house. It wasn't long after that when Lance discovered the pictures of many missing teenage girls. Add on Whitney's disappearance and subsequent murder, though her body had yet to be recovered, it was practically a nonstop true crime television series.

Shae's sudden appearance in town clearly rattled the responsible party into taking a calculated risk that had paid off in waves. Leaving the ankle boots Emma had been wearing the night she disappeared was sick and twisted, but the threat had been well received.

Was that why the son of a bitch was lying low? Or was it something else?

Had Shae gotten too close before that night?

It was something to think through on his drive home. Shae had been taking every precaution he'd asked her to take since she'd been staying with him. She was meeting his uncle in a public place with people who would watch out for her wellbeing. There was no reason to call in reinforcements, but what could it hurt to have either Noah or Lance stop in at the diner to pick up some lunch?

Jace had brought his Range Rover to a complete stop in the middle of the highway. He didn't hesitate to shoot a quick text to Lance, asking for the favor. Noah was most likely up at the lake with the Schaeffers working on those new cottages that Rose had switched contracts on with regards to the renovation companies.

Once that was done, he began going through the events of the afternoon he'd first arrived home. It was the same day that Shae had come to town, so who had she interacted with that would cause the killer to take such deliberate action and risk getting caught in the process?

The answer to that question brought him back to what his brothers believed this entire time—someone they all trusted and had known their entire lives was a murderer.

"AND YOU TOLD this to Sheriff Percy the next day?"

Shae had always known that Jimmy Webb had been an eye-witness the night of her sister's disappearance. For the longest time, there had even been rumors that Jimmy had been the one responsible. No one had proven otherwise, yet the community had somehow managed to sweep that accusation under the rug when it became too much to bear. After all, how could someone who'd been born and raised in Blyth Lake be responsible for something so evil?

"Yes, which is why Percy scoured those woods from top to bottom." Jimmy pushed away his lunch plate to make room for the coffee the waitress was about to set down in front of him. Sure enough, Molly was right there with the standard porcelain cream mug that had been a staple of this diner since the day it opened. "Thanks, Molly."

"Can I get you a cup of tea, Shae?" Molly's tone contained that particular pity Shae had come to loathe. She'd chosen the location due to the safety of the place, but she should have realized that meant word would get out and every seat in the diner would be taken for a chance to eavesdrop on her conversation. "I had Cassie get that English Breakfast tea you tried to order your first night here."

Cassie was the daughter of the infamous Annie Osburn. Both of their past deeds had been fodder for the gossip mill, so one would think they would take special care to treat others with respect. Who knows? Maybe that's why Cassie had ordered Shae's favorite tea.

"I'd like that, Molly," Shae responded with a tight smile, wanting more than anything to get back to her conversation with Jimmy. "With milk and sugar, please."

"Coming right up."

Molly departed, but her absence only highlighted those patrons sitting at the counter listening to every word uttered. Every click and clank of the silverware touching the plates of those eating lunch were amplified as everyone waited to hear what Jimmy said with bated breath.

"Shae, I drink. It's a known fact that I go on a bender a

couple of times a month." Jimmy took a sip of his coffee with no remorse in how he lived his life. He set the mug down with a thud. "I've spent time in jail. I wasn't the best son, brother, or uncle to my family. I've been divorced twice, and they've rightfully taken me to the cleaner each time. I own my mistakes, but let me make one thing perfectly clear. I know what I saw that night, and that was your sister walking down Seventh Street before—for some unknown reason—heading back into the woods."

"What do you think happened to her?" Shae asked, truly wanting his opinion. "My parents never got over the pain of losing her. At times, it seemed that they'd even forgot they had an older child. Not that I blame them. We all dealt with our grief in our own way."

"I think someone snatched her from that area, just as the police suspected from the get-go." Jimmy's face was leathered from years of drinking and working odd constructions jobs here and there in the blazing sun, but the disgust written in his features was unmistakable. "I've gone over and over that night, recalling each and every vehicle parked on Main Street and Seventh Street. There wasn't a car or truck that shouldn't have been there."

Shae understood what Jimmy was trying to convey to her, but she was still left in the dark as to who was responsible for abducting Emma. Jimmy believed there was someone walking among them whose soul was as black as the ace of spades.

"The cemetery is on that end of town, so I couldn't tell you if someone parked in the lot and got her out that way. Then there's the fact that she could have gone back to that bonfire. Who's to say one of those teens didn't do something they regretted, trying their best to get rid of the evidence."

It was obvious that Jimmy was waiting for her to deny that

scenario from the way he looked at her over the rim of his mug. He took a drink, which reminded her that Molly should be returning to the table with a cup of tea. Shae bought time before addressing his supposition, because she personally knew the majority of those teens in attendance that night.

A quick look toward the kitchen had Shae noticing that Molly was setting the tea bag, creamer, and sugar next to a steaming cup of water on a tray. Calvin, Harlan, and Chester were eating quietly at the counter. Sheriff Percy had a booth to himself in the corner, though she had to remind herself that he no longer deserved that title.

Miles Schaeffer was having lunch with his two older sons on the other side of the diner. Their relationship certainly hadn't been what some would say was on solid ground for quite some time. Given the fact that Clayton Schaeffer had almost burned Lance's house down with him in it didn't help matters any. Wes seemed to be the one keeping the peace. That wasn't surprising, given that Chad was nowhere to be found to do the job himself lately.

It was Billy Stanton's presence that bothered Shae the most. He was having lunch with Julie. It was common knowledge that the two of them were involved, but their newfound relationship was still mind-blowing. Julie had been distraught the day after Emma's disappearance, as had Brynn. They had both witnessed Billy admitting to the police that he had only danced with Emma that night because he felt bad for her to have such high hopes of winning him over.

Billy's behavior and disregard of the fact that a girl's life had possibly been in jeopardy was nauseating and something that Shae would never be able to forgive.

"Here you are, hon." Molly transferred everything on the tray to the table. She caught on to Shae's line of vision, though she didn't say a word about the rich kid trying to fit in with the regulars. "Let me know if either one of you would like dessert. Cassie just baked some apple, peach, and cherry pies."

Jimmy maintained his gaze on Shae as they both allowed Molly to leave without ordering a slice of homemade pie.

"Everyone accounted for one another that night, Jimmy," Shae reasoned, having gone over the statements of each individual multiple times over the years. "I realize they could have lied, but I would imagine a guilt like that would eventually rot a person from the inside out."

Shae had enough experience in her line of profession to know what that kind of *mistake* could do to a person psychologically. Now calculated murder? That was another exponential multiplier in and of itself several orders higher.

Shae began mixing in the right amount of sugar with a dollop of milk. She continued to come up with questions as she stirred the contents round and round.

"You mentioned that you were walking home from the Cavern." Shae tapped her spoon on the rim before setting it down on the plate. "Did anyone else leave around the same time?"

"No. There was only a handful of customers left. Jeremy Bell, of course." Jimmy rattled off a few names, leaving Shae to believe he was telling the truth by saying that night continued to haunt him to this day. "Miles Schaeffer. Harlan and Chester. Calvin left earlier that evening so that he could take his fishing boat out before the sun rose over the water. Tiny, of course."

"What about Byron Warner?" Shae recalled Jace mentioning that Byron couldn't drive into the city to provide Nick with a keg. It caused her to wonder why. "Was he at the bar that night?"

"I believe he and his father stopped in to have a drink for the old man's birthday, but they were out of Dodge well before midnight." Jimmy drained the rest of his coffee. "I can't tell you who is responsible, but I don't doubt that someone we all know took your sister and those other girls. I don't trust anyone in this town anymore, and neither should you."

Shae tried to stop Jimmy from reaching for his wallet, but it was of no use. He stood before tossing down a twenty and some additional ones to include a tip.

"Thank you for talking with me, Jimmy," Shae replied softly, wishing she had more questions and that he had some answers that made any kind of sense. Why had Emma gone back into the woods? Had she been meeting someone? "I do appreciate it."

"Anytime, Shae." Jimmy looked down at the floor in what Shae assumed was some type of regret from his follow up statement. "I don't speak to my nephews and niece, excluding the occasional greeting here or there. I know you and Jace are close. He's a good man. A lot better man than I am, that is for certain."

Shae wasn't sure what Jimmy was trying to say, and she never got the chance to ask. He lifted his ball cap from the side of his chair, adjusted it just so, and walked out the door. As if someone had let the air out of a balloon, everyone began talking at once. Not to Shae, but to each other in hushed tones.

The reprieve allowed Shae to drink the rest of her tea while going back over everything she and Jimmy had talked about during their lunch. She'd learned nothing new, but that wasn't unexpected. Jace had said weeks ago that Jimmy was drunk that night and couldn't recall anything other than seeing someone walking down Seventh Street. The way the rumor mill had churned, Jimmy could have either been the guilty party or he'd completely fabricated seeing Emma that night just for the attention.

After this lunch meeting, Shae didn't doubt Jimmy's honesty

about what he believed he saw that night. Emma had emerged from the woods only to turn around and run back in.

A jingle of the bell from above the door indicated someone entering the diner, and Shae wasn't all that much surprised to see Lance. She had honestly expected someone from the Kendall clan to stop in long before this point.

"You can tell Jace that I'm completely fine," Shae said with a smile, lifting her tea cup in greeting. "Your uncle left a minute ago. You probably saw him on the street. I was going to stop at the bar to see Brynn before heading back to Jace's house. Can I expect to see you there?"

"First, Jace is only looking out for your safety." Lance took the seat Jimmy had just vacated, holding up a hand toward Molly. He must have ordered takeout as a way to cover for his presence. "Second, Brynn is up at the lake visiting Rose. She wanted a second opinion on the paint picked out for those cottages she's having renovated."

The topic of the recent renovations up at the lake had Shae looking over Lance's shoulder toward the Schaeffers. It was a shame that Clayton had to go and ruin such a big contract. He'd panicked and made some poor decisions, all because he'd assumed Detective Kendrick might wrongly believe he was responsible for killing Whitney Bell.

"Every choice has a consequence." Lance had apparently swept the diner to see who was in the vicinity. He didn't appear the least bit empathetic to what the Schaeffers were going through. "It wouldn't surprise me if Clayton and Wes are losing quite a lot of business because of his recent arrest."

"You think they'll be asking Miles to take them back into the family business?"

"Maybe." Lance was holding out some cash for Molly as she handed him a bag with two Styrofoam containers. "It won't be easy, and they'll have to abide by his rules or hit the road. I know for certain that Noah won't take any crap from any of them."

If it was one thing about a small town, it was that everyone's dirty laundry was strewn all over for all to see. Shae didn't envy the Schaeffers the stigma of such family drama being the grist for the rumor mill.

"Like I said," Shae repeated, knowing full well that Lance would call Jace and let him know that she was safe and sound. "Jimmy and I had an interesting conversation, and now I'm going to hit the ladies room before heading home."

Shae cringed when she said that last word she'd sworn she would use in the proper manner. Jace's house wasn't her home.

"Drive safe, Doc."

Shae grabbed her purse off the back of her chair and headed toward the restroom. She utilized the facilities and was washing her hands when she could hear the telltale beep of her phone, letting her know that she received a text.

Taking the time to dry the water droplets from her hands, she eventually dug into her purse to find that she'd missed a call from her parents. The text was from Brynn.

Meet me up at the lake near Cabin Nine. I found some old photos that might be of interest.

Shae's breath hitched in her throat at the significance of the message, though she did try to contain her excitement. Nothing ever seemed to pan out for her when it came to finding new information pertaining to her sister's disappearance.

She quickly pressed the phone button that would initiate the call. Lance had mentioned that Brynn was up at the lake, but what kind of photos had she found while visiting Rose? While the line continued to ring, Shae tossed the paper towel in the garbage can and slung her purse back over her shoulder in her haste to hurry out of the diner.

Lance must have grabbed his order to go, because he was no longer sitting at the table. It was also interesting to note that most of the customers had paid their bills and left as well, especially seeing as they no longer had a conversation to listen to in order to gain some dirt.

"You've reached Brynn. Leave a message or you know where to find me."

Shae lifted a hand in parting to Molly, who was cleaning the used dishes off the counter. She used her left hand to open the glass door and stepped outside, instantly wincing at the light drizzle of rain that had come from the grey clouds above.

Great.

She left a brief message after the predictable beep, letting Brynn know that she was on her way. Shae dropped her phone into her purse so that it wouldn't get wet, exchanging one item for another. She quickly pressed the unlock button on the key fob and opened the driver's side door.

Old pictures. That could mean nearly anything.

Shae shouldn't get her hopes up, but a tinge of excitement ran through her as she turned the key in the ignition. There had been speculation lately that the summer camp was a connection between the victims, especially given that Sophia's body was found here in Blyth Lake.

What if there *was* something in those pictures that proved that theory right?

Would Shae finally get answers to the questions that had haunted her for the past twelve years?

CHAPTER TWENTY-THREE

JACE SLOWLY DROVE down his driveway, scanning the house and property line for anything out of the ordinary through the wipers swiping away the drizzling rain. It was only a matter of time before the skies opened up, but all seemed relatively peaceful and quiet.

He'd spoken to Lance earlier, who had done the favor of stopping in at the diner. He'd mentioned Shae had caught onto the reason for the to-go order, but that she seemed amused by his welfare check.

Jace had spent the long drive home thinking about who Shae had spoken to that first night who might have panicked at her presence. She'd been to the diner where Harlan, Chester, and their wives were having dinner. She'd mentioned days later that she'd already run into Jack and Calvin on the day she'd arrived, along with whoever might have been in the bar that night.

There was truly no way to know who became rattled due to Shae being back in town.

According to Lance, Uncle Jimmy had already left the diner by the time his brother had arrived. All seemed good on the safety front, and now they could spend the rest of the afternoon and evening enjoying each other's company.

Jace pulled up to the garage, though he made sure to park a little more to the left so that Shae would be able to pull out of the stall without a problem should she need to leave the house before him. He'd taken to having her use the garage for safety purposes.

He shut off the engine and then grabbed the samples of the lumber he'd chosen, wanting Shae's opinion on the color. It was more of a burnt red than the standard color used by most ranches. He pushed aside the fact that she wouldn't be here to see the finished product. There was no room for wishing the future could be different. He would play out the hand he was dealt, and not waste a second of precious time that he was being granted.

Jace got out of his Range Rover and jogged toward the porch in an effort to stay dry, making him wonder how much rain the northern part of Michigan got during the fall season. Lake effect must account for a lot of rainfall.

It had crossed his mind to see if they could initiate some type of long-distance relationship. He sure as hell wasn't ready for what they had to come to an end. Would she go for something like that? The more serious question was would he be willing to move to Michigan, thereby leaving his family—the same family he'd climbed mountains to get back to during his years in the service.

It wasn't something that needed answered now, especially considering they still had a week left. A lot could change in the course of seven days. Would it make a difference to Shae if Emma's abductor was found and answers to her disappearance finally solved? Would she be able to then come home...her true home here in Blyth Lake?

Jace slid his house key into the slot, twisting it until the deadbolt slid out from its lock. He pressed his thumb down on the lever and pushed open the door.

Instantly, he sensed the stillness in the way he'd done when entering an empty building over in Kandahar. There was a loneliness that hung in the air that was unmistakable. The incessant beeping of the security system also told him that no one was inside.

"Shae?"

Jace called out to her anyway. He didn't immediately react in a negative manner when she didn't answer. Shae had told him countless of times that she wouldn't forget to take the necessary precautions when it came to her safety. Besides, Lance had spoken to her at the diner. Jimmy had already left, confirmed by Lance watching their uncle's truck driving out of town in the opposite direction of Jace's property.

He punched the correct sequence of numbers into the panel before continuing into the kitchen, gently setting down the wood samples he'd brought home. Shae could have run into someone when she'd left the diner or simply chosen to drop in on someone for a brief visit. There was an easy way to find out.

Jace reached into the front pocket of his jeans and pulled out his phone, using his thumbprint to unlock the screen. Within seconds, he'd brought up Shae's name and initiated the call.

Only to have it ring four times and go straight to voicemail.

Jace didn't hesitate to call his baby brother.

"Lance, did Shae stop in at the bar to talk to Brynn?"

"No, though she'd planned to until I told her that Brynn was up at the lake," Lance responded, the shrill sound of a saw cutting over the line signifying that he was in the shop with their dad. "Shae said she was heading home. Why?"

"She's not here." Jace walked back through the house, having never set his keys down. He reset the alarm, locked the door behind him, and quickly took the porch steps, heading toward his vehicle. "She's also not answering her phone. I'm heading back to town. I'm sure she's fine, but we all know it's better to be safe than sorry."

"I'll give Brynn a call. She should be back at the Cavern by now. Maybe Shae went to the bar and waited for her there."

"Could be." Jace was in the driver's seat and doing a quick turnaround when he thought about something Shae said last night. He wiped away the drops of rain from his face. "She did mention she wanted to see Annie Osburn before she went back to Michigan. Maybe she's there. Listen, give me a call if she's at the Cavern. I'll stop at Annie's on the way into town."

"You know that she's not going to appreciate you traipsing all over town like she's an underage teenage girl who stayed out past her curfew," Lance said wryly, the quiet in the background telling Jace that his father was now listening to every word.

"True," Jace acknowledged, not concerned about Shae's reaction in the least. After all, she was a psychiatrist. It was for his own peace of mind that he have proof she was okay after the event three weeks ago. What professional could argue that sentiment? "I have a rational reason for that, though. Now go touch base with Brynn and call me back."

Jace disconnected the phone, waiting a moment for it to connect to the Bluetooth in the radio. The moment everything synced, he once more tried to reach Shae.

Four rings and voicemail.

An uneasy sensation ran down his back, similar to those times when he was in combat and the shit was about to hit the fan.

"Shae, call me back immediately when you get this message."

He resisted the urge to call Mitch, knowing his older brother had his hands full out at Raymond Dixon's ranch. Reaching out to Detective Kendrick was certainly an overreach, considering Shae was most likely visiting an old friend and that there was no cause for worry. That left Jace with driving through town and hitting up the residences where Shae would have gone to visit, such as Annie Osburn or even Jeremy Bell.

Jace stepped on the gas pedal, taking one of back roads a little too fast given the wet conditions. Even the thought of Jeremy Bell losing his daughter to the same son of a bitch that took Emma had all his crazy thoughts spinning out of control.

He did his best to quell the fear that was trying to rise up inside of him, having only one goal in mind—reaching Shae.

SHAE PARKED BY the cabin Brynn had mentioned in her text, squinting through the rain being swept away by the windshield wipers. It was raining harder than when she'd left the diner, making her wish she'd brought a light jacket. She'd certainly be drenched by the time she made it to the cabin.

Thankfully, Brynn held open the door so that Shae wouldn't be standing outside getting soaked while waiting for her to answer. She technically couldn't make out her friend's figure due to the rain and shadows from inside the cabin, but at least this signified she'd driven up to the right one. Cabins nine and ten were right next to one another and the plaques were rather aged through weather and time.

Shae suppressed a groan when she opened the car door, using her shoulder as leverage. She'd have to make a run for it. She palmed her keys and quickly shut the door behind her, not even bothering to take her purse. There was no use in getting the leather bag wet from the cold rain.

Splatters of raindrops hit her hair and shoulders first, instantly soaking through the material of her red blouse. The fabric was clinging to her skin by the time she'd made it inside. She laughed as she shook off the water, even pushing her hair back from her face.

"This weather is just awful." Shae wasn't surprised to see

that the furniture in the cabin had been removed for the renovations Rose had scheduled to have done to the older cottages. Her first thought was that Brynn had been in here to help with the choosing of paint colors and had inadvertently found more old photographs in one of the cabinets. "So, what did you—"

The jarring pain that sliced into the back of her head stopped her from finishing her inquiry. She tried to turn around to tell Brynn that something was wrong, that maybe she was having a stroke or maybe symptoms of an aneurysm, but she couldn't get her voice to work.

Help me.

The outer edges of her vision began to blacken as she tried to focus on something, anything that would keep her grounded. Something told her that if she succumbed to the darkness, she'd never see the light again.

That's when a pair of brown boots came into view, indicating to her that she was looking down at the floor.

Why was Brynn wearing work boots?

Right before the blackness swallowed her whole, the answer materialized in her mind and consuming fear flooded her senses. Brynn wasn't in this cabin.

Shae had walked into a trap, set by the one and only person who would want to do her harm—the same man who'd taken her sister and murdered countless other girls.

Shae was now at a serial killer's mercy…of which he had none.

CHAPTER TWENTY-FOUR

JACE RECALLED BEING pinned down in a village in Afghanistan, having been separated from the rest of his unit during an ambush on his convoy. They had exploded an IED on the gun truck directly behind his lead vehicle. Incessant gunfire along with the whoosh followed by a lingering hiss and subsequent booming sounds of RPGs hitting hard targets still resonated in his ears. The knowledge that it was only a matter of time before his vehicle was targeted had torn at his gut. Would he and his crew be able to avoid being captured? The fact that they needed to return had been all that had penetrated his mind.

Bottom line? It had been the most stifling sensation he'd ever experienced, almost as if a boulder had been set down on his chest to prevent him from breathing.

The only difference between then and now was that he wasn't fearing his own life…he was scared shitless that Shae was going to lose hers.

Four hours had passed since anyone had heard from Shae, either in person or by phone. Something bad had happened, and he hadn't been there to stop it. The alert had gone out and everyone was looking for her.

"We're tracing Shae and Brynn's cell phones now," Mitch said, walking into his office while removing the rain jacket he'd had on during the showdown with Raymond Dixon. "Brynn used it to touch base with Rose this morning about their visit, but she hasn't seen it since. It could just be a coincidence."

"Brynn made multiple stops. She checked in with Kristen at the bar, the diner to pick up a pie order for Rose, and then to the lake at Tiny and Rose's cottage," Lance offered, letting everyone know that somewhere along her path she'd lost her phone. Either that, or someone had stolen it. "Their cabin is on the north side of the lake, near the restaurant."

"And you tried the phone locator app?" Noah asked, his attention fully on the conversation at hand regardless that he'd been on his phone for the past five minutes. He was coordinating a search party for Shae through various people, including Reese. She was with Brynn and Gus, relaying pertinent information from the other residents involved. "What about Shae's phone?"

"Sheriff, both phones are turned off." Patty stood in the doorway, giving an update that was no help to Jace. He curled his fingers into the palms of his hands to keep from screaming at each and every one of them. He knew the odds. With each passing minute, the less likely it was to find a missing person. "But we were able to see that both devices were last pinged off the cell tower closest to the lake."

That was enough information for Jace. He'd been leaning against a filing cabinet, doing his best not to lose his mind, but he instantly made a shot for the door at this latest development. Patty moved to the side without hesitation, though all of his brothers' warnings were being vocalized. He didn't stop and proceeded through the door of the station out into the cold rain.

"Jace, what have you got?"

A quick glance to his left showed Detective Kendrick making a beeline for the sheriff's office. He was rushing forward in an attempt to avoid getting soaked. It was all but useless now that he'd stopped to talk to Jace.

"The last ping went to the cell phone tower up near the lake." Jace ignored the sound of the door opening behind him. "I'm heading there now."

"I'm having Patty pull the details on Shae's phone to see if she received any calls or texts," Mitch informed Kendrick, though Jace didn't break stride as he stepped down from the curb and to the driver's side of his Range Rover. "Jace, take Lance with you. Deputies Warner and Foster are scouring the county, looking for her Jeep Grand Cherokee. Noah is going to take a drive back out your way to see if maybe she ran off the road somewhere. Kendrick and I will follow you up to the lake."

"I have an officer heading out to Jace's residence, as well as two others taking a walk through the woods where Emma disappeared." Kendrick's words stopped Jace from actually getting into his vehicle. Reality had already hit home that Shae was likely in some sort of trouble, but to end up like her sister? He couldn't conceive such a notion. "This perp purposefully placed the boots Emma wore the night she was taken into Shae's room for a reason. It's not a stretch to believe he was trying to make a point."

Jace hesitated, allowing the rain to soak into his shirt. He'd gone back to his house to secure his firearm and was ready to face whatever came at him or to take down whoever had Shae. He couldn't allow himself to believe that she would end up like her sister. It wasn't going to happen. But Kendrick's suggestion that the son of a bitch might take Shae to the same place he'd abducted her sister wasn't unreasonable.

The locations were on opposite ends of town. Time was of the essence.

Which damned location should he choose?

Lance was already in the passenger seat, wiping the rain from his face. He'd go anywhere Jace wanted, regardless of the danger, as would the rest of his family. Noah was pulling out of his parking spot, quickly heading down the street with his given task.

What if Shae was somewhere in the woods? What if Jace was wasting precious time by driving out to the lake?

"We know one thing for absolute certainty," Mitch said over the crack of thunder rumbling across the sky. He was holding his useless rain jacket now that his clothes were soaked with rainwater. "She was at the lake after meeting Jimmy for lunch. We go where the evidence takes us."

Jace nodded, unable to get his words out around the constriction of his throat. He was betting Shae's life on a cell tower.

He yanked open the door and settled in behind the wheel, reversing his Range Rover out of the parking spot before Mitch and Kendrick even made it to the car. The wipers were already working overtime on high, and the roads were basically clear of any other vehicles as he drove them out of town at high speed.

"She'll be okay."

Jace wanted to believe Lance with everything in his power, but they were both aware of the tally of victims by this bastard. He'd gotten away with kidnapping multiple teenage girls for over twelve years, maybe more. Then there was Whitney, murdered and then hidden away like all of the other victims. What would make Shae the exception?

She was exceptional to him. In every way. From her cautious spirit to the purity she displayed when her guard was down. Her laugh was infectious, and she wore her heart on her sleeve. Shae would do anything for anyone, regardless of the cost to herself. She'd proven it time and again with the way she interacted with Calvin, Harlan, the Schaeffers, and anyone else who had some connection to the case. She'd even extended a hand to Billy Stanton, regardless that he was worth less than a piece of shit stuck on the bottom of a shoe.

"They say fear is crippling," Jace managed to say after clearing his throat a few times. He made a sharp right, taking the road that would lead them to the lake. He gripped the steering wheel tightly as he struggled to release his pent-up anger. "We dealt with it on a daily basis over a decade while we were fighting alongside our brothers and sisters. I'm not saying there wasn't a time or two that I didn't truly believe it wasn't my time, but I was at peace with myself."

Lance rested a hand against the dashboard as Jace took a turn in the road faster than intended, though the tires held fast to the wet road. He pressed the gas pedal a little more in hopes of gaining every precious second that he could, given the circumstances.

"This type of fear?" Jace could barely contain his sanity at the thought of what Shae could possibly be experiencing right at this moment. "It gives clarity. It provides a lucidity that makes all the world's problems disappear in the blink of an eye."

"I've been there, Jace." Lance's shaky breath told Jace that he wasn't just saying platitudes. He'd heard what had happened when Clayton Schaeffer tried to torch down Lance's house…with him in it. But it was witnessing Brynn standing in the middle of the grass soaked with gasoline that had turned his world around. "I know what you're experiencing firsthand, and you can alter any decision about your future you feel is necessary once we get her back."

Future? It was hard to think past the present when they were on borrowed time.

"I love her, Lance," Jace admitted, not ashamed in the least when his voice caught in his throat. "I love her."

CHAPTER TWENTY-FIVE

THE POUNDING PRESSURE mixed with the sharpest of pains in the back of Shae's head was what initiated her consciousness. The nausea was overwhelming, but it was the cold, damp sensation that began her uncontrollable shivering.

"Stop."

Shae was relatively sure that her plea didn't cross her own parched lips.

She was swinging, the front of her banging against something solid. It was the air leaving her lungs in one long rush when she was thrown down onto her back that had the horrifying memories returning of her entrance into the cabin.

Someone had hit her from behind. It hadn't been an aneurysm or some type of stroke. She'd been lured up to the lake so that she could be the killer's next victim. How many times had she visualized talking to the man responsible for her sister's abduction? Unanswered questions had cost her countless sleepless nights, and the constant wishing that she had a face-to-face with Emma's killer.

Her chance was finally here, but she didn't believe it would work out the way she'd dreamed over the last twelve years.

Shae forced herself to open her eyes, thankful her head was turned to the side so that the raindrops didn't impair her vision. Her previous queasiness returned tenfold when the structure she was laying on began to rock back and forth.

They were on a boat of some kind, and the sun had set. Either that, or the storm above was severe enough to block out the sunshine.

What was lying next to her near the front seat? A thick silver chain and a cement block materialized as her brain finally accepted her fate. It was then that fear began to spread its tentacles as her mind became more lucid toward her environment.

Who could be this sick and twisted?

She still had no idea who was responsible for hitting her in the head and dragging her out onto the lake, but there was one thing she knew for certain—she was going to die if she didn't get off this damned boat.

Where was he?

Shae tried to lift her head, but any movement immediately brought about waves of nausea. She couldn't even move her arms, for they were tied behind her back with either duct tape or something else she wasn't able to break free of by attempting to pull her wrists apart.

The rhythmic thud finally broke through her haze, as if a sign from above.

The boat was still docked, and it was hitting the pier.

Shae forced herself to open her eyes once again, searching for any sign that he was near. Had he left her all alone? The sight of someone leaning over the side of the boat and untying the rope from the pier came into view. She couldn't tell the identity of the man, not unless she purposefully called for his attention.

He would kill her here and now.

Of that she was certain.

That left her little recourse but to try and escape without him noticing, but she was running out of time. And it wasn't like she could get out of the boat without him seeing her. He was literally four feet from her, and she had no doubt that he would finish the job quickly and efficiently.

Shae would have given anything to call a time out and somehow stop this all from happening. No matter what she did in this moment…she was likely going to die. She bit back a sob, wishing the pain in her head would subside for just a few minutes. The throbbing agony made it hard to think things through.

Jace…what would he think happened to her? Would he be left wondering for years and years if she were alive or dead? Would he suffer the same fate she had over her sister?

Shae wasn't being given time to make the decision on whether or not to satisfy her haunting need for answers, or prevent Jace from suffering the same destiny. It wasn't fair. He was a good man. Honest, loyal, and caring to a fault.

Was it possible to love someone in the short amount of time they'd been together? She'd seen many things over the course of her career, and one thing always hit home in regard to her patients. Nothing mattered more than one's happiness in their time here on earth.

She'd had every intention of leaving Jace and heading back to her life in Lansing…where she went through the daily motions of living. Her sister had been robbed of life by this man's hands, and yet Shae had been willing to do it to herself.

No. She wasn't ready to die. She wasn't ready to leave Jace, and those answers she sought most of her life weren't more important than the man she wanted to spend the rest of her life with.

Shae almost waited too long in making her decision, for the man in the yellow rain slicker turned to face her. At the last second, the rope must have caught. He leaned over the side of the boat, giving her the precious time she needed to hoist herself up. It was difficult, considering her hands were tied behind her back and the head injury made it hard for her to concentrate. She managed to stand on wobbly legs all the same.

If only she could see the man's face before she let herself fall backward into the cold water, but the rain was incessant in its torrent. The sound of her slipping off the edge must have caused him to spin, but her vision wasn't clear enough to make any type of identification.

She didn't even bother to scream as she plunged into the darkness, the lake swallowing her whole. Had he charged forward to try and catch her? Or did he already accept that she was dead, because she had no use of her hands and no way to swim?

A coldness unlike any other enveloped her, almost as if she were being wrapped in a malevolent cocoon.

Shae didn't bother to fight the pull of the bottom, her heavy soaked clothes taking her down, down, down until her hands touched the sandy bottom of the lake. She grabbed ahold of the slippery vegetation, doing her best to hold on so that she didn't float back up to the surface. It shouldn't be too deep where the pier was located, but it was profound enough that he couldn't reach her by leaning over the side of the boat…unless she floated to the surface.

The longer she held her breath, the worse the pain in her head became. It was only a matter of time before her body would force her to inhale. She still had use of her legs, so she did the only thing she could—she kicked as hard as the water would allow so that she was forced away from the boat.

She couldn't swim, but she'd be able to use her legs to try to get herself toward the shore. Pushing off the bottom one more time allowed her to put a little distance between herself and the boat.

Would it be enough?

Shae didn't have time to answer that question as her lungs began to burn from the lack of oxygen and her inherent need to breathe. She was going to have to come up for air. Had she pushed herself in the right direction? Would she be able to surge to the surface using her legs or had she gone too deep into the lake?

Her heart was beating so hard against her rib cage that it sounded like miniature detonations were being set off in her ear drums. She hadn't even realized her eyes had been open in the minute or two she'd been submerged under water until lightning streaked across the sky above, giving her hope at how close it appeared.

Hope.

Jace.

The two were now connected in a manner she'd never thought possible, but it gave her enough determination to bend her knees and push with all her might. Her lips were open to take in as much as possible the moment she broke the water's surface, while she kicked her legs furiously to try and keep herself upright.

Shae immediately sought out the boat and could have screamed in anguish when she realized her mind and body had been tricked by the lake's underwater effects. She was no more than ten feet away from *him*.

The barely lit sky behind him made up of storm clouds all but made him an ominous silhouette. He still wore the rain slicker with the hood over his head, preventing her from even getting a glimpse of his identity.

Did it matter? She was likely to die in the next few minutes.

The rain was coming down even harder, splashing against the water and causing her to blink furiously to keep her line of sight clear. He was pointing something toward her, though she couldn't quite make out what it was until a wired net landed right in front of her face.

It was a fishing net.

A hysterical sob rose up in the back of her throat, making it hard for her lungs to make up for their lack of oxygen. The muscles in her legs couldn't keep up with the amount of strength needed to maintain her upright position. No matter how hard she twisted her arms, the binding around her wrists wouldn't budge.

She was losing the battle of her life.

Instinctively, she lurched back from the net so that the thick wire only caught the side of her face. She bobbed in the water, but she managed to lay on her back so that she could frantically kick and propel herself inland.

The start of the boat's engine told her that he was more likely to reach her first than she was to make it to shore. Shae screamed as loud as she could to give herself the needed incentive to move her legs even faster, not willing to accept that she was to die in this lake.

As if the universe answered her plea, two divine lights came out of nowhere.

CHAPTER TWENTY-SIX

J ACE AND THE others had spent the last half an hour scouring every section of land around the lake, starting with the restaurant. Deputies Warner and Foster hadn't found Shae or her vehicle in their search of the town. Noah had been unsuccessful in backtracking to Jace's property. Brynn, Reese, and Gus had struck out on all the other properties on the outskirts of town Shae might have driven to for one reason or another.

Kendrick's men were still searching the forest near Noah's property, but the current consensus was that she hadn't been taken into the woods. The detective had already called in reinforcements, along with K9s, to help search the wooded areas and the properties surrounding the lake.

Jace held the keys that included a master key to each and every cabin overlooking the water. He was working only on mechanics at this point, because he'd had to shut down every emotion that wanted to consume him over the past four hours. The amount of rage coursing through his system would only waste what precious time Shae most likely had left.

"Cabins nine and ten are next," Lance called out over the roar of thunder above as he headed toward the Range Rover. Only fifty or so yards separated each group of cabins along the west side of the lake, but the brush and trees made it nearly impossible to see one pairing from the next. At this point, they were taking two at a time before moving on to the next. "I think this row ends with twelve."

Jace couldn't allow this stretch of cabins to end, because that would mean she'd be lost to him. There would be no other hope given to him that she could be brought home.

The vibrations of the cell phone in his pocket had him quickly pulling out the device regardless that it was pouring down rain. Hell, both he and Lance were soaked through to their skin, but that was meaningless at a time like this. All that mattered was having Shae back in his arms where he could protect her from whatever evil haunted this town.

"Tell me you found her," Jace managed to say without breaking stride. He rushed to the driver's side door. Lance was already in the vehicle. "Is she—"

"Cabin nine! You're closer, but Shae's cell phone provider just emailed Patty a string of her last texts. The son of a bitch used Brynn's phone and told Shae to meet up at cabin nine."

Jace rammed the key into the slot and turned the ignition until the engine burst to life. He yanked the gear and shifted it into drive, having thrown his cell phone at Lance. He had one goal and one goal only—to reach the cabin.

Hours had gone by.

Would Shae still be there? Would she even be alive?

Jace couldn't stop the various images of what he might find once he barreled through the door. How was it humanly possible to physically hurt so much at the thought of losing someone? He now had a new respect for his father, because now he under-stood the anger and grief that had consumed the man for the past three years.

"…heading there now. Do you think there's a possibility she could be on the lake? It's been a while since…"

Bits and pieces of Lance's conversation broke through Jace's concentration. The tires were spinning so fast that they were having trouble grasping the pebbles. The wipers weren't working fast enough as the rain kept pummeling the vehicle, but he could still make out the two cabins where Shae was last known to be…only her vehicle was nowhere to be found.

He wasn't wasting time, so he drove the Range Rover right over the grass and was about to brake so that they would be directly between the two cottages when Lance called out a directive that Jace desperately needed to hear.

"There!" Lance pointed and jabbed a finger into the windshield. "Someone's on a boat near the pier."

Jace's gaze immediately made contact with the yellow rain slicker. His two headlights cut through the pouring down rain and had caught the edge of the pier. Someone was on a boat, and he or she had risen their arm to shield themselves from the brightness.

Neither one of them knew for sure that this individual was responsible for Shae's disappearance, but it was all they'd gotten in the endless hours they'd been searching. Besides, who the hell would be out on the lake in this weather? It was a death sentence.

He didn't hesitate and stepped on the gas, causing the Range Rover to go over the small decline. The quicker they reached the boat, the faster they would have their answers.

Please let Shae be on that boat.

Please let Shae be on that boat.

Jace repeated that mantra over and over until he had to stop the Range Rover feet from the edge of the pier.

"Fuck!" Jace slammed the vehicle into park and hastily opened the door, watching in horror as the boat began to recede into darkness. He took off at a dead run with every intention of running down the pier and diving into the water. He couldn't allow that fishing boat to get too far out, or else he'd end up losing Shae. "Lance, call Mitch! Tell him the boat is heading his way!"

"Jace, stop! There, in the water."

It was too late for Jace to brace himself against the wood of the pier. He was already in midair when Lance's words penetrated through the panic of doing whatever was necessary to stop that fishing boat.

Wasting any time could literally cost Shae her life, if she wasn't dead already.

The water was damned cold, but that didn't prevent Jace from doing what was necessary. He trusted his brother. He trusted all his siblings, so when he broke the surface, he quickly scanned the water to search for what Lance had seen in the beams of the headlights.

There!

Movement in the water toward the shore, but then it was gone in the blink of an eye.

Damn it!

Jace looked over his shoulder, already having lost sight of the boat. The fading rumble of the engine all but told him that it was impossible to follow behind, leaving Mitch the best chance of catching that son of a bitch.

Was Shae on the boat or had she been left behind to drown?

Jace didn't waste any more time. He began swimming toward what he and Lance had both seen, already knowing that Lance had run into the water. The ripples coming from his brother's actions made it all but impossible to locate the original area where they'd both seen movement.

He'd seen a lot of crap happen while serving his country, but he'd also witnessed countless numbers of miracles. What happened next would absolutely qualify for the second category.

Someone broke the surface, gasping and coughing, struggling for air.

Jace and Lance both moved at the same time, but Jace reached her first.

It *was* Shae. And she was alive.

"I've got you, Doc." Jace brought her back toward him, holding her tight as relief overcame him to the point of tears. He wasn't sure if it was the rain, water, or his emotions that were running down his face, and he didn't give a damn which one it was. She was safe. "I've got you."

He realized very quickly that her hands were bound behind her back. First things first, though, and that was getting her on solid ground. She'd still yet to say a word, which had sparked another bout of fear inside his soul.

"Lance, go get a blanket out of the back of my vehicle and call Mitch." Jace shifted so that he could effortlessly pull Shae from the water. Within seconds, he had her on the shore. "Doc, talk to me. Are you—"

Jace cut off his question when he recognized the familiar stickiness on his hands when he'd cupped her face to look her over. She was bleeding, and it was everywhere.

"Lance!" Jace's brother had already made it to the Range Rover to retrieve the blanket, but it wasn't nearly enough. "I need light! And bring the first aid kit!"

Jace kept murmuring soothing words that everything was going to be okay when he knew nothing of the sort, but he refused to allow her to think for a second that she wouldn't recover from whatever trauma she'd received from that sick fuck. Shae's teeth began chattering, telling him she was close to going into shock…if she wasn't there already.

"You stay with me, Doc. Don't you fucking close those brown eyes of yours, do you hear me?" There wasn't a chance in hell he was letting her fade away now. "Fight against the darkness, baby. You can do it."

The best thing would have been to get her into the back seat of the Range Rover, but he wasn't sure he should move her any more than necessary. The rain was still coming down, but until he could see the extent of her injuries, they'd have to suffer through.

"Mitch called for an ambulance. He, Kendrick, and every other available armed person is scouring the shoreline for that boat." Lance dropped to his knees and tossed Jace the first aid kit while quickly unfolding the blanket. He arranged it so that the material covered the lower half of her. An umbrella came out of nowhere, which he then held steady over her head. "Let's see what we got before transporting her to the vehicle."

"I-I want t-to stay."

Jace's heart squeezed when Shae's words made no sense. *Damn it.* She was hallucinating, but it couldn't have been from hypothermia this soon. It was cold due to the rain, but it wasn't nearly cold enough to cause the onset of symptoms already.

"Here."

Lance had grabbed a flashlight instead of taking the time to move the Range Rover. The first thing both of them were made aware of was the gash alongside her cheekbone. Blood was running down into her hair in uneven rivulets as her teeth continued to chatter.

"Doc, we need to get you to a hospital," Jace told her gently as he continued running his trembling hands down the length of her, even moving the blanket to make sure she didn't have any fatal wounds. He'd always prided himself on having a steady hand during combat, but the thought of losing her was almost his undoing. "Let me just—"

The back of her hair was matted, enough to know that the

injury had taken place hours ago. The rain or water from the lake was what had caused the wound to reopen. Head wounds were notorious for bleeding profusely, which was proven by the amount of blood on his fingers. The sight was enough to jar him back into survival mode. She might have a severe concussion. That was most likely the reason for her slurred speech and general lack of awareness.

"Head injury, but her neck seems fine." Jace tossed the wet blanket to the side and scooped her up into his arms, grateful that Lance still held the umbrella so that she was able to keep her eyes open without fuss. "Shae, you're going to be fine. Do you hear me? We're going to get you to the hospital where the doctors are going to fix you right up."

Lance and Jace, who carried Shae in his arms, managed to slog their way through the wet sand and dirt to where the Range Rover waited for them. Never once did Jace stop reassuring her that all would be okay. Lance opened the back door so that Jace could lay Shae down on the back seat with her feet elevated. He was more concerned with her slipping into shock than the scalp wound at this point.

"Drive," Jace ordered, as he slammed the back door. He ran around the other side so that he could see just how severe her head injury was so that he could convey her wounds to the emergency physicians who better be waiting on hand. "Call Mitch. Tell him we can't wait for the ambulance, but the staff should be waiting for us with a gurney when we pull up outside the emergency room."

Jace had put on the dome light so that he could see the damage. Ever so carefully, he lifted her head and turned her in such a way that it wouldn't hurt her to lay down on his lap.

Lance had already turned on the heat full blast, regardless that the outside temperature was most likely in the high sixties.

The rain had brought in a cold front, and their soaking wet clothes didn't help any.

Jace reached behind the seat, knowing he had left a jacket in the back at some point. He quickly found it and laid the thick coat over the top of her to capture whatever heat he could maintain around her. Her teeth were still chattering, but she tried her best to look up at him.

"Don't talk. We're going to get you to the hospital."

"I w-want to s-stay."

"I know," Jace soothed her, not wanting to get her worked up when her body needed to rest. "I know you do, Doc. But you're hurt and we need to get you fixed up, okay?"

"Jace, I'm c-cold and my h-head hurts like hell, but y-you're not l-listening to me." Shae had attempted to grab his hand, but she rested her palm against her temple. It was better than touching the wound in the back. "I w-want to stay w-with you. Here. H-home."

"Okay, baby," Jace managed to say, grateful that she hadn't asked for the moon. He would have been on his way to NASA if she had. This request? This was doable, because he had no intention of letting her out of his sight after this. Would he have gone to Lansing, Michigan? Absolutely. "You're home. I'm home. We're never leaving again."

"…her to the hospital. Did he try to dock anywhere?"

Jace half-listened to his brother ask questions regarding the bastard who'd hurt Shae. It wasn't that he didn't want to know the outcome, but her health was more important right now.

"Doc, I need to see how bad your head wound is," Jace explained, helping her shift so that she was looking at the back of the driver's seat. She maintained one hand on her head and then wrapped the fingers of her other around his wrist. "Squeeze as hard as you need to, Shae. I know this hurts."

Jace moved away her matted hair and was able to see the gash, but it wasn't nearly as bad as what the amount of blood indicated. Again, head wounds were notorious for bleeding profusely. There was no doubt she had a massive concussion, but the injury was hours old and had only started to bleed once more due to the water dissolving the clot.

"Okay, baby. Turn back toward me so that I can look into those beautiful eyes of yours." Jace's Range Rover always did have an amazing heating system, so the inside had all but turned into a sauna. That didn't stop her teeth from chattering completely, but it did slow it down. "You're going to be fine. We're going to get you to the hospital, and the doctor is going to stitch you up in no time."

"He h-had a cinder b-block and chains," Shae whispered, her lashes drifting toward her cheeks. She quickly opened them when he stroked his thumb across her forehead. "He w-was going to d-dump me in the w-water."

"You're safe, Shae." Jace couldn't stand to see her wince as agonizing pain must have cut through her head with every word she spoke. "Lance, drive faster."

"Y-you don't u-understand." Shae licked her lips and closed her eyes tight when she shifted so that she was holding his hand. "I think E-Emma's there, t-too. I th-think they're all in the l-lake."

CHAPTER TWENTY-SEVEN

"**Y**OU SHOULDN'T BE here."

Shae had heard the same line about fifty times in the last hour. Jace had every right to be concerned, given the massive headache that was currently throbbing against her temples, but she wouldn't be anywhere else than right here at the lake where she truly believed Emma had been dumped like discarded garbage.

"As long as I have you and that cup of tea you're about to hand me, I'm good."

Two days had passed since Jace had found her drowning in the water near cabin nine. She'd had twenty-six stitches put into the back of her head, including having a special glue that sealed the cut on her cheek to lessen the scar that would be left behind. The plastic surgeon that the emergency staff had brought in the other night couldn't understand why she wasn't more concerned about the possibility of scarring, but Jace had been there to take care of everything.

He'd been more than supportive, and every kiss he gave her reminded her that she'd survived.

She made the choice to live in the present, not the past.

"You shouldn't be so selfish." The small smile and gentle kiss to her forehead told her that he was joking, though only half so. He would absolutely lock her away at home, if he thought he could get away with it. "I'll get the drinks."

Shae allowed Noah to help her sit on the tailgate of his truck, Brynn and Reese already in attendance. Their silence said everything they were thinking and feeling as they grimly watched the events unfold in front of them.

It was time Emma was finally laid to rest.

Detective Kendrick was currently overseeing numerous diving teams, not wanting to drag the entire lake if it wasn't necessary. If what they believed to be true was in fact correct, there was more than one body weighted to the bottom of the lake. Preserving whatever evidence remained was crucial, not that much could survive in the water for twelve years. This had more to do with possibly of discovering Whitney among the bodies, who would have been one of the last known victims.

"…of them. From the looks of the crowds, downtown must have closed every shop."

"…checked on Calvin? He…"

"…found the boat in the middle of the lake. It was just sitting there…"

"…Shae's vehicle? Was it ever found or…"

Numerous conversations by various people in close proximity were talking with one another, going over the events of the past two days. Shae had been released from the hospital a few hours ago, but she'd had Jace stop by Calvin's place on the drive up to the lake. He was no longer a suspect, considering that he'd been alongside members of the search party all evening. But he was still quite shaken to find out that his boat had been the one used to try and take her out to the deepest part of the water.

"Kendrick is having a forensics team go over the boat inch by inch. If there's so much as a partial print, they'll find it."

Noah was deep in conversation with Lance about the fact that the authorities had located the boat on the north side of the lake. It had been anchored and abandoned, the assailant long gone.

"I ran into Mitch this morning," Lance shared, taking one of the coffees that Jace had gotten out of the Range Rover. He was balancing two trays worth of coffees, a Coke for Brynn, and a hot tea for her. She gave him a reassuring smile when his gaze met hers. It didn't seem to ease his concern. "They figured the son of a bitch swam to shore near the restaurant. He must have bided his time to walk out of the area on foot or he's got a place on the lake."

The information Lance was relaying wasn't anything she hadn't already known after speaking with Jace, who'd been in close contact with both Mitch and Detective Kendrick. Shae, in turn, had communicated everything to her parents. They had taken yesterday to make arrangements to come to Blyth Lake and were in the process of making the drive today. She'd assured them that she was fine, but as a psychiatrist—and more importantly, as a daughter—she believed it was in their best interest to be here when the lake was searched.

Shae hadn't known at the time that Detective Kendrick was going about this investigation very carefully, using diving teams at certain depths of the lake that would be ideal to hide the bodies. It was downright creepy to know they'd been swimming in what was basically a graveyard for the past twelve years.

"Here you go, Doc." Jace had finished dispersing all the drinks, leaving a coffee for him and a tea for her. He tossed the two to-go containers in the back of Noah's truck, ignoring a sideways glance of irritation from his brother. His expression gave way to sympathy when his gaze landed on Shae. "Hey, don't get your feathers ruffled. No one feels sorry for you. There isn't a single person in this town that doesn't admire how you held your own against that bastard."

"You mean the state, and it might very well be the country, if the national news was anything to go by," Gus interrupted, holding up a copy of a newspaper as he joined them overlooking one of the diving teams. He had a toothpick in between his lips and a ball cap to shade his eyes from the early afternoon sun. "Charlene Winston finally got her national headline, and it appears she was spot on in her reporting, even guessing the right amount of stitches you received."

Shae wasn't surprised at the length Charlene Winston had gone to in order to get her facts right, even going so far as to probably pay one of the hospital's employees for Shae's medical records. Jace, on the other hand, appeared ready to take matters into his own hands.

"What's done is done," Shae said softly, wishing the dull ache in the back of her head would dissipate at some point today. Her oversized sunglasses helped keep the sun out of her eyes, but it wasn't nearly enough to take the edge off. "I'm not worried about reporters, journalists, or anyone else for that matter."

"Is that your new sidekick?" Gus asked, purposefully keeping things light to keep her emotions in check. Honestly, Shae could cry one minute and want to laugh hysterically the next. She chalked it up to her head injury, and not the fact that today might be the day she would finally discover her sister's resting place for the last twelve years. "I have a feeling this one will be glued to your side until this is all said and done."

Shae didn't bother to look over her shoulder, knowing full well it would cause her head to hurt even more than it did now. Gus was talking about the officer Detective Kendrick had assigned to her for the duration of this investigation. He'd pulled some strings and now had three shifts watching over her every eight hours. It was true this investigation was now getting national coverage, and the governor didn't like being on the front page being shown in a bad light.

"They have the necessary credentials." Jace leaned against the side of the tailgate where he was able to wrap his arm around her waist. "I had an old buddy of mine run a…"

"This will help, you know," Reese said softly, drowning out the conversation between Jace and his father. She rested a hand on Shae's knee in comfort. "I don't know what I expected to find by coming here to Blyth Lake, but it certainly wasn't my cousin's body. A part of me wanted to believe so bad that Sophia did run off to California to live out her dreams, but the funeral we were able to give her left me with a peace I hadn't experienced in eleven years."

"I'm not so sure that I know how to feel any other way," Shae shared reluctantly, still grateful to have found a new friend who could understand the toll of what today would bring. "Regardless, my parents deserve that peace you speak of. I can only hope that today is the day it's delivered."

The next hour passed by uneventful, with most every resident in Blyth Lake either congregating around the available shorelines or parking alongside the roads to get a glimpse of the search. The media crews had set up shop in the early morning hours and hadn't budged from their positions, their cameras constantly rolling in case something or someone was brought up from the depths of the lake. There was even a helicopter or two that kept making passes, though they were careful not to get too close to prevent creating unnecessary waves in the water.

Shae was resting the side of her head against Jace's shoulder when she finally realized he was holding something in his hand. She reached out, taking the small rectangular item from his loose grip. The burnt reddish hue told her exactly what it was that he'd brought with him today.

"I love it." Shae ran a thumb over the rich color, liking it better than the routine red used for barns around these parts. She could easily picture Jace out front of the new stable, giving riding lessons to the younger generations. He'd even mentioned hiring on a few veterans in the area once he got the business up and running. "It will go beautifully against the white-washed corral paint you chose the other day. Of course, you're going to need a hundred gallons or more to do all the fences covering all sixteen acres."

"There's a horse ranch around forty minutes from here that's selling a couple of younger mares. I just need to find the right stud. Think you'll feel up to taking a drive that far at the end of next week?"

Shae understood what Jace was really asking, and it had nothing to do with buying a horse. Facing death had a way of putting significant details of one's life into perspective. She'd told him two nights ago that she wanted to stay here in Blyth Lake…with him. And she'd meant it from the bottom of her heart.

"I'll go anywhere with you, Jace Kendall." Shae was once again unable to control her emotions, though she made an attempt. She'd be glad when the concussion symptoms receded, because she was relatively certain this was worse than meno-pause. Then again, her mother might disagree. "I don't know what the future holds for me in terms of my career. I might open my own practice or I may decide to stick with the hospitals closer to the city. I'll be leaving my parents in Michigan, and I'm honestly not sure they'll ever come back here to stay. But Blyth Lake *is* my home. *You* are my home. I've fallen in love with you, Jace, and there's nowhere else I'd rather be than here with you."

Shae had no doubt that everyone had heard her declaration, but they all understood this was a private conversation between she and Jace. He stepped in front of her, wedging his way in between her legs while blocking the sun. She didn't stop him from lifting her sunglasses, allowing him to see the vulnerability, honestly, and hope shining in her eyes.

"I need you to know that I'd move anywhere you need me to in order to make this work." Jace gently cupped her face, careful of the cut on her cheek. The warmth radiating from his touch was something she'd come to rely on, and he didn't disappoint now. "Home is where you are, Shae. Nowhere else."

"Your mother wanted you to raise your children here, and this is where Emma will be laid to rest when we find her." Shae truly believed they were both meant to return to the hometown of their childhood. "Blyth Lake *is* where we belong."

"Jace, Shae," Gus warned after stepping closer, his attention somewhere in front of them. "Something's happened."

Jace shifted to the side so that Shae could see Mitch and Detective Kendrick walking side by side in unity to deliver some type of news…although it was already a given from their grim expressions. She laced her fingers with Jace and squeezed, her heart accelerating with the hope of finally finding what she'd come home for almost a month ago.

"First, your vehicle *was* dumped in the lake. The DNR has boats out there right now and they'll recover the vehicle as soon as possible to prevent the petroleum products from contaminating the water. More important, the divers have so far counted fifteen bodies on the northeast end of the lake in the deepest part out about one hundred and fifteen feet down. I've called in the FBI, who will be here within the hour. They'll bring in their own forensics team to retrieve the remains." Detective Kendrick's sympathetic gaze landed on Shae. "We won't know the identities of all the bodies for the next few days, if not weeks. But I'll make sure the special agent in charge has your phone number, Ms. Irwin."

Shae nodded, though her throat constricted at the overwhelming news they'd finally discovered the victims who'd suffered unthinkable deaths. She'd had to swallow quite a few times before she was able to get her words out to thank both him and Mitch for seeing this investigation through to this point. Regardless that the FBI were being called in, she had no doubt that local and state authorities would be available day and night. After all, they all had a personal stake in bringing the person responsible to justice.

"Emma's here," Shae whispered, believing with all her heart that her sister would finally find peace in her final days of rest. She shared a heartwarming smile with Jace. "She is, and we need to bury her next to my grandparents."

"We will, Doc," Jace promised, pulling her closer and surrounding her with love. "We'll bring your sister home, and we'll find out who's been using our town as a hunting ground. It's high time this nightmare was brought to an end and the killer is forced to pay."

~ The End ~

Thank you so much for reading Jace's book in the Keys to Love series! Don't forget to pre-order Gwen's story—Unlocking Shadows—releasing in September 2018.

www.kennedylayne.com/keys-to-love-book-four-mdash-unlocking-shadows.html

Gwen Kendall spent ten years in the Navy and used the last four to create a life for herself she could be proud of away from the confines of her overprotective family. Being the only woman in the Kendall clan tended to be a bit overwhelming at times.

Chad Schaeffer had been hired on to help restore an old farmhouse for one of the returning Kendall siblings. He'd heard about the trouble the family had encountered and honestly didn't want to go anywhere near their properties. He had a change of heart when he saw the most recently returned Kendall sibling stepping out of her car with a key in her hand.

Gwen had waited a very long time to have a place to call her own, just as she had waited for the right man to share her life. One night of seduction convinces her she's found both, but someone wants to take it all away. It's been said that old houses retain a piece of each person who has lived there, but she never counted on the dark shadows wanting a piece of her.

Books by Kennedy Layne

Keys to Love Series

Unlocking Fear (Keys to Love, Book One)
Unlocking Secrets (Keys to Love, Book Two)
Unlocking Lies (Keys to Love, Book Three)
Unlocking Shadows (Keys to Love, Book Four)
Unlocking Darkness (Keys to Love, Book Five)

Surviving Ashes Series

Essential Beginnings (Surviving Ashes, Book One)
Hidden Ashes (Surviving Ashes, Book Two)
Buried Flames (Surviving Ashes, Book Three)
Endless Flames (Surviving Ashes, Book Four)
Rising Flames (Surviving Ashes, Book Five)

CSA Case Files Series

Captured Innocence (CSA Case Files 1)
Sinful Resurrection (CSA Case Files 2)
Renewed Faith (CSA Case Files 3)
Campaign of Desire (CSA Case Files 4)
Internal Temptation (CSA Case Files 5)
Radiant Surrender (CSA Case Files 6)
Redeem My Heart (CSA Case Files 7)

Red Starr Series

Starr's Awakening & Hearths of Fire (Red Starr, Book One)
Targets Entangled (Red Starr, Book Two)
Igniting Passion (Red Starr, Book Three)
Untold Devotion (Red Starr, Book Four)
Fulfilling Promises (Red Starr, Book Five)
Fated Identity (Red Starr, Book Six)
Red's Salvation (Red Starr, Book Seven)

The Safeguard Series

Brutal Obsession (The Safeguard Series, Book One)
Faithful Addiction (The Safeguard Series, Book Two)
Distant Illusions (The Safeguard Series, Book Three)
Casual Impressions (The Safeguard Series, Book Four)
Honest Intentions (The Safeguard Series, Book Five)
Deadly Premonitions (The Safeguard Series, Book Six)

About the Author

First and foremost, I love life. I love that I'm a wife, mother, daughter, sister… and a writer.

I am one of the lucky women in this world who gets to do what makes them happy. As long as I have a cup of coffee (maybe two or three) and my laptop, the stories evolve themselves and I try to do them justice. I draw my inspiration from a retired Marine Master Sergeant that swept me off of my feet and has drawn me into a world that fulfills all of my deepest and darkest desires. Erotic romance, military men, intrigue, with a little bit of kinky chili pepper (his recipe), fill my head and there is nothing more satisfying than making the hero and heroine fulfill their destinies.

Thank you for having joined me on their journeys…

Email:

kennedylayneauthor@gmail.com

Facebook:

facebook.com/kennedy.layne.94

Twitter:

twitter.com/KennedyL_Author

Website:

www.kennedylayne.com

Newsletter:

www.kennedylayne.com/newsletter.html

www.ingramcontent.com/pod-product-compliance
Lightning Source LLC
Chambersburg PA
CBHW060430180626
46817CB00007B/2752